Plagued: The Rock Island Zombie Counteractant Experiment

WATCH OUT FOR BULLETS.

Plagued States of America, Book Two

Better Hero Army

Ev '14

All contents copyright © 2014 by Evan Ramspott. All rights reserved. No part of this document or the related files may be reproduced or transmitted in any form, by any means (electronic, photocopying, recording, or otherwise) without the prior written permission of the publisher.

This book identifies product names and services known to be trademarks, registered trademarks, or service marks of their respective holders. Better Hero Army and Evan Ramspott are not associated with any product or vendor mentioned herein.

This is a work of fiction. The characters, incidents, and locations portrayed herein are fictitious, and any similarity to or identification with the location, name, character, or history of any person, product, or entity is entirely coincidental, except for the characters of Curtis Matt, aka "Matty" – who is secretly Matt Baha – and Danielle Kennedy. Thanks for their encouragement and support.

ISBN 1-495-22945-9
ISBN-13 978-1495229459

First Printing: March, 2014
10 9 8 7 6 5 4 3 2 1

Cover design by Kendall Roderick
Cover copyright © 2014 by Evan Ramspott

For soldiers…
…and the zombies they protect

"Readily will I display the intestinal fortitude required to fight on to the Ranger objective and complete the mission, though I be the lone survivor."
- *From the Army Ranger Creed.*

One

It may as well have been a death sentence. Drawing a red card was bad enough. It meant eighteen months of service patrolling the safe side of the Moaning Coast, but to find a big letter D in the top right corner? Defensive duty. Holding the wall. Front lines. Fodder. Call it anything. Everyone who drew the card knew what it meant. Death just waiting to happen. Or worse, getting turned.

"So, we got ourselves another hero," Game Warden Mitchell said, not returning Mason's salute. Mitchell sat behind his elaborate cherry wood desk with its formal calendar mat and silver-embossed name plate, a spit-shined, silver pen holder sprouting only two pens, and a standard number two pencil, point up. The cigarette burned near its end on the lip of a plastic ashtray.

"No, sir," Lieutenant Mason Jones replied, still holding his rigid salute.

"Huh?" the warden asked quickly, glaring at Mason—a young man, not yet thirty. All muscle and no brains, that's what the warden was probably thinking. Typical Army. Well, not typical. Mason Jones had to have four things in his background to even be considered for this duty. He had to be a medic, he had to have seen combat duty, he had to be an expert in hand-to-hand combat, and he had to be a Ranger. The warden glanced over his file. Lieutenant Mason Jones was all that and more.

"No, sir, I'm not a hero," Lieutenant Mason Jones replied stoically. "I have not earned any such commendations."

"Oh, a funny guy, huh?" Warden Mitchell asked, picking up his dying cigarette to take one last drag. It was so quiet in the room Mason felt certain he could hear the crackling of the tobacco turning to embers.

"I did not intend—"

"Shut up and sit down, Jones," the warden interrupted, waving toward the chair. Mason looked at him, still holding his salute, unmoving. Warden Mitchell smashed out the cigarette and blew the smoke in the air toward Mason, then leaned back in his chair.

"At ease, soldier," Warden Mitchell said. The young man continued to stand rigidly, his hand at his eyebrow, holding it there and waiting. He'd wait until summer. "Jesus, Jones, you're not going to make too many friends around here like that," Mitchell said, waving his hand to his eyebrow in a nonchalant salute.

Mason nodded, withdrawing his salute and widening his legs to stand at ease, both hands behind his back.

"Sit down, lieutenant," the warden said, indicating a plush chair. Mason glanced at it, then back at the warden. "That's an order, actually," Mitchell told him flatly.

Mason nodded again and took the seat.

"Says here you've been transferred to me to fill my outgoing hardship," Mitchell said, holding up Mason's file. "Apparently Banks' wife is better at blowjobs than mine and got some Senator to sign his get-out-of-jail card. And lucky you, just coming off your second tour of duty in Hotter-than-hellistan, you pick up his remainder. Five months." Mitchell put down Mason's file, staring at the young lieutenant suspiciously.

Mason said nothing.

"I find it interesting that this just happens to coincide with the fiasco at Biter's Hill last month," the warden went on, staring intently at Mason for any sign or twitch or eye movement that would give him away. "A little too convenient our Big Brother sending you here to finally relieve someone who's been begging to get out since before he got here," Mitchell continued, still prodding. "Don't you agree?"

"Sir," Mason replied. It was put neither as a question nor affirmation. "Is it possible that I might file for a hardship discharge, too?"

"You *are* a fucking comedian, aren't you?" Warden Mitchell snapped.

"No, sir," Mason replied. "I'm just trying to serve my last six and go home."

"Well, this is your home now, Jones," Warden Mitchell said with disgust, plucking a pen from his jar and signing the orders in Mason's file. He closed the folder and shoved it across the desk, waving a hand over his eye as way of salute. "Dismissed, lieutenant."

"Yes, sir," Mason replied, standing abruptly with a rigid and proper salute. He took his file from the warden's desk and went for the door. The warden glared suspiciously at the young lieutenant as he left.

Two

Lieutenant Mason Jones taped the red card to the inside of his locker alongside the small mirror. At least this wasn't barracks living. He had a room, even if he was sharing it with another lieutenant. A second lieutenant named Thompson, who wasn't here. He was on duty somewhere on the wall or in the prison itself. Maybe patrolling the market, who knew? Mason only knew he was not only assigned a "D" red card, but that he was also put on the graveyard shift. Graves. In a zombie prison.

Newbies always got the worst duty. Mason had been around long enough to know that rule. He had to cut his teeth, prove his worth, and prove his allegiance. He thought it funny that in every new situation they considered torture a method of solidarity. That was fine. He could take a little torture.

"You ready?" Sergeant Chavez asked while knocking on the open door. He looked at Mason's duffle bag, how it was only half full. Mason hadn't brought anything with him except uniforms. Personal items were inspected coming over the bridge, so he left them all behind rather than have any taken.

"Yeah," Mason replied distantly. He picked up the duffle bag from the bed and shoved it into his locker. He could unpack later. He still had orientation to sit through.

"You officers have it nice here," Chavez said as he led Mason down the hall. He pointed out the day room and the big screen television. "The nearest chow hall is across the street, and it's a good one. Don't miss breakfast."

"You mean dinner?" Mason asked.

Chavez only grinned.

Outside, Chavez hopped into a Jeep and turned the engine over. Mason fell into the passenger seat and Chavez lurched forward, taking a wide U-turn as Mason buckled himself in.

"That's the south wall there again," Chavez pointed out as he cruised east. "It used to be Beck Street or something, but the water level has everything past it five feet under. It's all motion sensor and video surveilled. Officers don't pull tower duty, but so you know, anyone caught climbing the walls gets shot a hundred times before they'll stop to ask questions." Chavez followed the sharply curving wall northward. He accelerated to an intersection, slammed on the brakes, and pointed east past a guard shack and wooden gate stretching across the road. The guard shack reminded Mason of the check points he manned from time to time in Egypt during his tours there, except there were no cars coming or going. Just one bored soldier kicking at the wall of the shack to keep from going crazy.

"The Meat Market is down there where the country club used to be. Lucky bastards. This is Rodman Road. We truck the biters in and out of the market along this route. Civilian traffic goes through check points all up and down East Avenue. This is East Avenue, by the way, sir. They blew the Rodman Bridge along with every other bridge up and down the river, so the only way off the island to either side is at the prison. You came through the Rurals access bridge coming in this morning. I'm going to take you to see the other bridge."

Mason didn't like hearing it said like that. The *other* bridge. The one leading to the Plague States, biter territory, or just plain hell. That same uneasy feeling he had his first day in Egypt crept up on him, an emptiness that came with disorientation to a world unlike any he'd known or experienced before. Just as then, Mason did the only thing he could. He let someone else lead the way. Chavez lurched the jeep ahead again, turning west hard. Mason held the door frame to keep from spilling out.

"These are all the barracks," Chavez said. "I live in that one," he added, pointing to the third on the right. "It's nice enough." He shrugged. "We've got chairs on the roof. In the summer you can look out over the river and almost believe you're home, you know?"

Mason only looked at his driver and guide. He couldn't imagine thinking home looked anything like this. But then again, he hadn't been here six months either.

Chavez, Rudy. Sergeant. Nine months into his tour of duty in Egypt, his team was ambushed during a routine convoy. All were killed except him. His life was spared due to being thrown from the vehicle into an abandoned shanty. Chavez dressed his own wound, and held his position against rebel opposition with only an M-9 for protection until helicopters arrived. They sent him here as reward.

The Game Warden was not much different than Chavez in that regard.

Mitchell, Robert A. Staff Sergeant, retired. Served two tours before retiring from the Navy Seals. He went to work for Blackline as a high ranking consultant, and wound up being an enlisted man telling generals what to do in the Middle East. He pissed off the wrong people, though. He was later transferred to corrections for two years at Leavenworth, and then sent here. Still, Mitchell was in charge of this place, as bad as it was, and that earned him some kind of respect.

Chavez pointed northward as they cruised along the road. Mason glanced at the long

Quonset huts, row after row of them.

"We guard *those* too," Chavez said only loud enough for Mason to hear. Mason thought it odd the way Chavez said it, as if he was worried others might hear. Chavez glanced between Mason and the road a few times.

"Munitions?" Mason asked.

"And then some," Chavez said while shaking his head. "You've been briefed on the rule, right sir?"

The Rule: In the event of a breach of containment, after all other measures to arrest the advancement or escape of detainees are exhausted, and at the orders of the base commander or from a higher command outside of the facility, the use of Tactical Defensive Explosives shall be implemented to prevent further spread of the contagion.

"I know it," Mason said.

Chavez pulled up to the main gate of the prison, the one they called the Inside Passage—a man-trap with six-inch thick iron doors on both ends of the containment zone. Chavez honked his horn several times.

"Rudy, can't you just buzz us like everyone else?" a voice asked from a call box beside them.

"Open the door. I have fresh meat!"

The door lurched with a creak of protest, grinding aside to reveal a dark passageway that could fit an entire bus. Chavez drove inside and slammed on the brakes as he killed the engine. The door behind them stopped, and then began to roll shut. Blacklights glowed over every white surface, even the edges of Chavez's eyes. Mason figured his own eyes and teeth would probably glow white too.

"Kind of spooky, huh?" Chavez asked. "Try coming through with some biters sometime. Their eyes light up."

Chavez's teeth glowed as he smiled. A loud buzz announced the next gate was opening. Light from outside washed away the shadows and eerie glow of his guide's teeth and eyes. Chavez turned the engine on again and drove through the second gate straight toward one of three lone doors on the concrete building beyond.

Chavez killed the engine and hopped out of the Jeep, tossing the keys on the front seat.

"Aren't you worried someone will take it?"

"Where would they go with it?" Chavez asked with a shrug. "Welcome to the prison complex," Chavez went on. "We keep all the biters in here, from pre-registration through post-quarantine. The non-infectious ones we ferry back and forth to the country club through that roll up gate and loading dock."

Mason looked up at the concrete prison complex, a menacing structure that reminded him of the high school he attended, a similarly huge concrete building in the middle of a concrete jungle, and as a teenager he hated getting out of his car every morning once he arrived. He always felt watched. Judged.

"Don't forget your ID anywhere. I like these arm badge holders." Chavez turned the plastic armband over to display his ID on his upper arm, over his sleeve. "If you're caught without ID, they'll hold you for hours just to mess with you, to make sure you don't forget it again. Sometimes they put you in a cell down with the biters if you piss them off."

At the door marked three, Chavez rubbed his armband over a black sensor embedded in the wall. It beeped and the door latch clicked. He tugged the door open and motioned for Mason to enter. It was another man-trap, but this one was white and well lit.

"Try yours," Chavez said, pointing to the next door. A sensor blinked quietly next to the door handle. Mason pulled his ID card out from a cargo pocket and swiped it. The door unlatched and let them pass.

"May as well keep it out, sir," Chavez told him, pointing down the hallway. "You're going to need it a couple more times." There were several closed doors lining the hall with one large one at the end. Beside the door was a shielded glass wall with a counter. Above the door a sign read CHECK WEAPONS BEYOND THIS POINT.

"I don't have a weapon," Mason said as

they marched down the hallway.

"Oh, no, sir. This is where they give you one. It's your responsibility to check that you have one if you're going in. Don't ever go in without a sidearm."

"Should I sleep with one?"

"I do," Chavez replied.

Three

"So you're my new man," Captain Sanchez said as Mason entered the office. Sanchez immediately returned Mason's salute and held out a hand. "Glad to have you on board, son."

"Thank you, sir," Mason replied sharply, shaking the offered hand.

Sanchez, Luiz. Captain, Naval operations, assigned to the U.S.S. Delaware nuclear attack submarine for eight years. In a compression accident, he lost his hearing in one ear and was transferred to shore duty. Volunteered for both his previous and current tour on Rock Island.

"Is Chavez treating you well? Showing you the ropes?"

"So far."

"Good. Have a seat," the captain said, pointing at a chair across from his desk. Sanchez fell into his own chair, rubbing between his eyes. "I have a problem with you, Jones. You're the only Army officer on Biter's Island. I've got Navy and Marine officers coming out my ass, but Army's never sent me an officer for this post. I don't know what to do with you, to be honest."

"You could always send me back, sir," Mason replied.

Captain Sanchez didn't laugh. Instead he stared at Mason's uniform, at the Lieutenant insignia on his collar, the medic symbol on his arm, the Airborne patch on his front pocket.

"You're the fresh meat, Jones," Captain Sanchez said at last. "I only have grunt jobs on graves at the moment. If I were to put you somewhere else, well, it wouldn't look good."

"I understand, sir. I've been through it before."

"I'll bet," Sanchez murmured. "Your file has a few discrepancies I'd like to ask you about."

"Discrepancies?"

"Like where have you been for the past nine weeks? Your last tour ended abruptly. It shows you've been home for months."

"I took leave, sir."

"What?" Sanchez asked, cupping a hand over his good ear.

"Leave, sir. I took leave."

"Nine weeks?"

"No, sir. After I got my red card I was sent for additional training."

"What kind of training? You've got all the qualifications you need to guard biters."

"I had a medical refresher. I had to requalify for combat water survival, my fast rope, then—"

"None of that's in here," Sanchez replied, holding Mason's file in the air between them. "I don't know why you were picked for this duty, Jones. You're going to be mopping up shit out of biter cells for the next six months. Why the fuck would they send me a lieutenant for that?"

"I don't know, sir," Mason said.

"Huh?"

"I don't know, sir."

"That makes two of us. I recommend you get some R&R today. Your first shift begins at 21:30 hours tomorrow night. Chavez will fill you in on the check-in process and uniform requirements. Dismissed."

Four

Lieutenant Mason Jones looked over the steel railing surrounding the wall. The young Marine manning the machine gun emplacement beside him glanced nervously toward Mason. Another Marine held a pair of binoculars to his eyes and scanned the distance, trying to appear occupied even though he was equally curious. A lieutenant, they were probably thinking, coming to inspect things. Looking down the three story drop, Mason felt the full force of the prison complex.

Rock Island Prison Defense Facility, built by Breckenrock Corporation immediately following the outbreak, was planned as a holding location for recently infected human subjects, initially for the purposes of study. It was designed to hold over six hundred occupants in 426 cells. It was comprised of five levels, three above ground and two below. Medical laboratory units were constructed in the sub-levels. There were no windows on any floor, only five ground-level exits, one underground exit, and three above-ground exits, one of which was a roof access point for defense and airlift support. The outer wall was built a year later to prevent free access to and from the Plagued States without passing through the prison defenses.

Chavez stepped up beside Mason and looked down with him. The old 24th Street Bridge stretched over the slow moving river with its wide and vacant platform. It had several barricades in the form of steel gates that spanned its entire width. Mason thought it to be a flimsy defense to keep out the zombie horde, but with the gun at the rooftop as it was, the chances of anything making it across in one piece were slim. The road on the other side of the river disappeared, descending into abandoned buildings and overgrown forest.

Mason turned his gaze north to see the way to civilization over the 2nd Street Bridge, which was configured with another barricade system, this one of low concrete slabs to act as obstacles to slow crossing vehicles. The machine gun didn't face north, though. The barricades weren't to keep the people on the other side out. They were there to keep the people on the island in. Just to be sure, there was enough barbed wire lashed to the sides that birds made nests in the web.

Both bridges had a guard house that looked a lot like the checkpoints in the Middle East. He expected to see the black scars of past explosions studding the concrete, stretching toward civilization, but there were no such blemishes. It was a clean, empty expanse.

When coming to the island, they routed everyone through x-ray machines on the civilized side and made them surrender anything remotely resembling an electronic device, including radios, cell phones, cameras, and even Mason's electric shaver. They didn't want photos from this side getting out.

"At ease, Corporal," Mason said as he came closer to the mounted machine gun.

"What a shit hole, huh, sir?" Chavez asked and spat over the edge. "I like the other side of the island better."

"How do you get guard duty on the wall?" Mason asked Chavez.

"You don't want it, sir." Chavez replied, shaking his head and backing away from the edge. "Hardest thing to do is stare at freedom all day knowing you aren't allowed to go near it. It just sucks ass."

Mason sighed, standing straight and looking at the powder blue sky with its long streaks of gray like claws raking the atmosphere. *What a shit hole indeed.*

"Have you ever fired this?" Mason asked the gunner.

"Yes, sir," the corporal manning the gun replied. "We test it twice per month."

"I meant on biters."

The corporal turned to look at Mason,

gauging him, then looked at Chavez. Chavez nodded. "All the time, sir."

"How do you know they're biters?"

The corporal seemed confused by the question. He was a young kid, probably only a year out of high school, and on his first assignment.

"It's OK," Chavez said, stepping next to the gunner. "Move over and let the lieutenant have a look through the scope. Take a look, sir. We have signs posted all along the tree line. Every week we get out there with weed whackers and cut back the growth. We have fences further back guiding anyone who stumbles into our area toward the road or the river. Look right there, sir. See that structure? It's a phone booth. Pick up the receiver and we don't shoot you. Everything else is fair game. And we keep it lit at night.

"Rabbits love the chopped grass, so we get lots of them, and that attracts dogs and wolves, and they make a bloody mess back in the shadows, and the smell of blood eventually draws in a biter from time to time. If hunters are on duty, they go catch them. If not, then we get to pick them off. You should come up here and try it sometime."

"No thanks," Mason replied. "I've had my fill of killing."

"What, biters?" the corporal asked as though the notion were absurd. "They ain't people no more."

Mason stood and looked over the top of the gun toward the old, abandoned town in the Plague States, wondering if it would ever be possible to restore it. "Well, there's a lot of debate about that, actually," Mason put in, stepping away from the machine gun. "Carry on, gentlemen."

Five

The rest of Mason's orientation had been unsettling, but uneventful. After unpacking his duffle bag, he went for a jog. Based on the stares he received from civilians and soldiers alike, he figured there wasn't a very strict adherence to any fitness programs. It didn't matter to Mason. He enjoyed running. It helped to clear his mind, to ground him in the reality that even though this place was foreign to everything he knew of the world, the ground beneath his feet struck with the same consistent impact as anywhere else. There was no greater weight on his shoulders here except for what he piled on in his own mind. Thankfully, running helped shed him of those pounds too.

On his approach to the Meat Market he hardly realized what was unfolding ahead of him. The roadway abruptly ended into a huge dirt lot filled with enormous trucks the size of troop transports, every one outfitted in a manner that suggested the end of the world was near. The vehicles, generally long flatbeds with four-wheel drive, had numerous built-in pens of varied size and design. Some had large pens meant for storing several occupants, while other configurations of individual occupancy were abundant, appearing as rows of cages only about the size of a phone booth. Even the smallest of vehicles had room for ten detainees.

Mason jogged around the vehicles on the river side of the lot and around a stand of trees to find himself on a resort beach front, except instead of sand there was well-maintained, lush green grass. Ahead of him stood a lavish, wide building that looked like a golf course clubhouse with a broad wall of glass facing the river, outside of which was an enormous patio area with tables and chairs under umbrellas, all enclosed behind a wall of clear Plexiglas.

A three-story building stood behind the clubhouse, the only hotel on Biter's Island, complete with a casino that took up the entire first floor. This was where all the civilians were forced to stay, although most of the hunters preferred sleeping on their own rigs most nights.

This remarkable feeling of civility faded quickly. He passed behind the hotel and came upon a field of cages ringed inside of an enormous compound of chain-link fencing. Stretched high overhead was an assortment of sails laid flat to keep the majority of the interior of the marketplace shaded. Trucks backed up to a loading bay as though delivering goods, and a long line of people stood about in an orderly, although impatient fashion, waiting for names to be called and zombies to be handed over.

It was good that he had a chance to approach it alone rather than plunging in with an escort like Chavez. The Meat Market was the kind of place that needed to be seen several times to be believed. Aside from Biter's Bend, there was probably no other place on Earth quite like it. Mason's trained, stoic expression of military bearing fell prey to utter surprise. He donned the tell-tale widening to his eyes – that gawk of the uninitiated.

That was all Mason surveyed on his first pass of the area. He kept jogging and in a few minutes passed behind the Quonset huts Chavez had pointed out earlier. He was curious about their contents, but didn't stop to look around. They were built in the wrong configuration to be a sentry ring. If anything, blowing them all next to each other as they were configured would result in a massive crater. Their hinged roofs, however, hinted at their true design, and Mason hoped he would never see them yawning open.

On his second loop of the island, he watched zombies being moved from a truck to their pens. The pens were like chain-link dog runs, all joined together to make an oval ring, with four wide lanes into and out of the center of the compound. Inside the ring were kiosks and other temporary looking structures where words like Registration and Bidding Agent were displayed. Most of the biters were docile, easily moved. One struggled. It pulled from its handler, a kid of no more than eighteen. Onlookers in and around them stepped back, but didn't seem overly concerned. The handler got a better grip on the noose pole and drove the zombie's head downward to control it.

"Hold your pole, new-fag," someone shouted, and several hunters laughed. The handler was red faced as he yanked on the zombie mercilessly. The zombie snarled, its hands gripping the pole cinched below its chin. Mason kept running to avoid seeing the outcome.

On Mason's third pass, he slowed to listen to the nearest slaver hock his merchandise. "Fully domesticated," the slaver shouted. "One hundred and sixty pound male, all his fingers and toes. Slab trained."

Slab trained. That was the slang used to mean that the zombie could be trained to do certain tasks using the reward system, just like a good dog, with the reward typically being small slabs of meat. It meant it knew the clicker, the sound used at feeding time.

Mason slowed and approached the fence with his hands on his hips, trying to catch his breath as quickly as possible. Spaced at regular intervals around the pens stood a soldier in black with his rifle facing down across his chest. Behind him on the fence were two poles with nooses on the end, the kind Mason had been trained in before coming here, the kind used for catching zombies by the neck to subdue and control. Mason put his hands on the fence and stared through, fingers clutching to keep himself standing. His legs felt weak, but not from the jogging. Hard memories tried to latch onto his mind. This looked like Egypt all over again with its fences inside of fences inside of more fences, except over there the soldiers faced an angry crowd that herded young women in front of their men to advance on the consulate. There, they strapped bombs to little boys and made them run at the fence. There they did everything they could to get inside.

Here, it was apathy. Even the biters didn't seem to care about the chain-link barriers. What kind of degeneracy could lead to this? It had only been ten years since the zombie outbreak, nine since the containment was assured and the laws regarding the capture and sale of specimens for scientific research were passed. Then came knowledge of how to make the contagious no longer infectious, and someone had the bright idea to pass the reusability laws in order to help re-indoctrinate victims, and in no time, slave trading returned to American soil. Two states, then three, then seven. Mason came from one of those states. Ohio. One of the split-states. Part of its soil inside, the other part outside of the channel used to prevent further spread of the consumption pathogen. Ohio. *The* political battleground of American ethics.

"You'll have to back away," the nearest soldier said as he walked toward Mason. The young soldier had one hand on his rifle now and was waving for Mason to step back. Just like Egypt, a futile gesture when the crowd knew they weren't allowed to shoot. Mason felt like a foreigner, unable to decipher the soldier's words or the purpose of all this.

"Sorry," Mason said, taking his hands off the fence and backing away.

"Where's your I.D.?" the young soldier asked. He was a corporal, another Ranger.

Mason dug it out of the cargo pocket of his trousers. He was only wearing a brown t-shirt on top with no insignia or markings. He could be anyone, after all. How was the corporal supposed to know? Mason held up the badge, the blue bar of his I.D. apparent, indicating that he was an officer.

"Oh, sorry, sir," the corporal said, although his hand didn't budge from the grip of his rifle.

"No problem," Mason said. "Carry on."

Mason looked into the compound one more time and scanned the faces. All the zombies shared an expression of vacancy. Most were backed into the corners furthest from the sun, hiding under the corrugated rooftops. Even in the shade, they were still half-blind, and maybe even afraid. He wondered if zombies knew fear – aside from the fear they fed on, that is.

Six

"This is Matty," Sergeant Phillips, the night duty officer, said as way of introductions between Mason and his trainer. Matty was a big man, bordering on overweight, with equally heavy and labored breath. "Matty, this is your new partner."

"I thought you were fucking joking earlier," Matty snapped at Phillips. "You're really giving me a West Pointer? Banks was a complainer, but at least he'd push a broom!"

Mason stood silently, caught off guard by the outburst. Even though Phillips had said Matty might get upset at first, and based on Matty's unorthodox dress—the only military issue piece of clothing seemed to be his boots—Mason shouldn't have been surprised. From what Mason already knew, the big man didn't seem to care about military bearing.

"Matty, Lieutenant Jones was next in line. He got a red card just like everyone else."

"Yeah, like hell. He was supposed to go to the Hill, I'll bet. Sending him here instead? Why couldn't you assign him to the wall or gate duty? What the hell kind of shit is this, giving Banks a hardship and then sending me a cad-idiot? Shit," Matty said, shaking his head while walking out of the room.

Phillips stood behind his desk and sighed. He looked over at Mason and smiled weakly. "He likes you."

"I can see that," Mason replied.

"Come on, weak dick," Matty called from outside of the office. "Work ain't getting done by itself!" Softer, but obviously loud enough for everyone to hear, Matty added, "It'll probably only be me getting it done, though."

Phillips raised a finger. "Try not to get on his bad side right away, if you don't mind, sir."

Mason nodded and followed Matty down the hallway as the big man grumbled and complained.

Matt, Curtis aka "Matty", Petty Officer, Second Class, second demotion. After eight years as a Navy Seal with spotty performance reviews with regard to relations with superiors, he got into a fist fight with four Air Force Combat Controllers during an all-branches field training, hospitalizing three of them. He received a demotion and four months in jail. Upon successful rehabilitation, he returned to active duty only to get into several other small altercations, such as shooting out the tires of a Hum-V because—as PO Matt claimed in the report filed—"the son of a bitch nearly got them all killed by his driving. I'm doing the service a service keeping him off the road." PO Matt was transferred to Rock Island after an incident with a base commander's son, which resulted in the commander's car being pushed into the golf course pond while the boy was found tied to a tree. PO Matt was on his third consecutive eighteen-month tour on Rock Island. As far as seniority went, PO Matt beat the next nearest soldier by two years.

"So you're the new-fag, huh?" Matty asked angrily. "Did they give you the tour already?"

"They showed me—"

"Good," Matty said. "It's simple shit. We start on the top floor and work our way down. Biters aren't potty trained, so we get the luxury of hosing out their cells every night. They know enough to pull down their pants, but they shit on the floor. When they have more room, they pick a spot and keep using it over and over again. That's how hunters find them out in the world. In the prison, though, there ain't enough room. Just like dogs in a kennel.

"So we trap them, hose them down, hose down the cell, then squeegee it dry so they don't injure themselves when we let them go. Nothing worse than injuring the merchandise. The hunters get all bent out of shape when their precious zombies have bumps and bruises."

"We go in with them?" Mason asked as Matty swiped his card at the stairwell.

Both the door and Matty groaned. "Ah,

Jesus, don't tell me a Ranger's afraid of a few cock-biters." Matty tugged the door open and the fans rushed air over them. Matty stepped into the stairwell, shaking his head.

"I thought you said we start at the top," Mason pointed out. The duty officer was on the third floor.

"Ain't no biters on the third floor right now," Matty told him. "Shit, hardly any biters in the pens at all. I've never seen inventory so low. All on account of what happened at the Hill."

Biter's Hill, a township established inside the Plagued States immediately following the Flood Control Project. The city wall and waterfront had been constructed by the Army Corps of Engineers in an effort to establish a controlled region for safe landing of military and scientific personnel. After the Federal Rezoning Act made it unlawful for U.S. citizens or corporations to own property within the boundaries of the Plagued States, Breckenrock Corporation filed for a long-term lease and built the below-ground prison facility. For the past eight years, Biter's Hill had been one of three federally sanctioned zombie sales control points, until four weeks ago when it was destroyed following a major zombie prison escape, which overran the town. There were only twenty-nine survivors, eight of whom were rescued several days later from Scott Air

Force Base, over 100 miles away.

Mason and Matty emerged on the second floor. Mason felt overwhelmed by what he saw. He side-stepped and circled while moving toward the center of the room as though performing a reconnaissance of the area. He wasn't sure what to look for first. Everything clashed for his attention. The moaning was drowned by the sheer crime of the scene. Had he stepped back into Egypt? It appeared as though a bomb had rattled off as they stepped in, his ears still ringing from the concussion, his senses not quite recovered.

The center of the room was where the burning vehicle would have been if this were a street. Bodies should have been strewn around it with scorched earth and pock marks from shrapnel everywhere. Instead, he found an operating table standing at a forty-five degree angle, bloodied from end to end. The blackened earth surrounding it was instead a chaotic shower of blood, with stains that were pools in some places, smeared lengths in others as though bodies had been dragged off, with foot prints in blood everywhere.

The shock subsided and he began to hear again. The moaning was different on this level. It wasn't hunger like he heard everywhere else. Instead, it was the dull groan of constant pain. It sounded more like Egypt than he cared to admit.

"Fucking gruesome, huh? That Doctor Miller is a drunk-ass, sloppy surgeon."

"Do they slaughter pigs in here or something?" Mason asked incredulously, carefully stepping around the smeared blood stains streaking the floor.

Matty laughed. "No, this is how Doctor Miller likes it, though, the sick bastard. Thank God he's got a job cutting up zombies, because out in the real world he'd be on a CNN manhunt, for sure."

Even though Mason knew the salivary gland was the point of infection, and that the way zombies were neutralized for domestic labor was to surgically remove the glands, he never imagined it was done like this.

"How are we going to clean all this?" Mason asked.

"What do you mean *we*, white man?" Matty replied with a raised eyebrow. He let Mason squirm a moment before chuckling and walking toward a door that had the words JANITOR CLOSET on them. "Come on, weak dick, I'll show you what we gotta do."

Seven

"Hot damn, first floor," Matty said enthusiastically as he slid his card over the door panel. It chirped and the magnetic door lock clacked to let them in. "We might actually get out of here by five or six for once. This is the easiest floor. Just shit patrol in the cells."

Mason yanked the door open and they stepped through a fan-blast of wind to be met with the loud moaning of the zombies held on this level. They sounded normal, that constant plea for food as though constantly starved. Both Mason and Matty stopped and stared at the three figures standing between the rows of cells ahead of them. None of them wore uniforms. Two of them were putting something into a black and red case. The third began walking toward them. He was wearing a brown leather jacket, had long hair with streaks of silver at the temples, and a fake smile.

"Gentlemen," he said loudly, holding up his security badge to Mason. Mason realized it was because he was the only person wearing a uniform. "I'm Marcus Holden. We're authorized to be here tonight."

"I don't give a shit," Matty replied. "Get the fuck out of here before I shove those cameras up *all* your asses. You ain't filming us cleaning up shit again, you got me?"

The man named Marcus held up his hands innocently, his smile still fixed to his face. The two others stowing the camera gear had closed the lid on the black and red cargo box and began wheeling it toward the door. Both wore lab coats, and one was a woman. Mason looked her over for her badge as she approached. Matty had words for all of them, his verbal abuse hurrying them through the door, but not before Mason could read the scientist's badge.

Kennedy, D.

Mason stared at her as she passed. She glanced at him and her eyes registered a flicker of recognition, or maybe he had read it wrong and she was just concerned over the intensity of his stare. She was a tall black woman with long, tightly curled hair that appeared several shades lighter than should have been natural. Her bright red lipstick stood out against her white lab coat. Beneath the coat she wore a blue top and black skirt. All civilian attire. She didn't look back as she walked through the door, in her hand a cell phone in a pink shell. *Flaunting it*. Nobody was allowed to have a cell phone on the island.

"Who were they?" Mason asked once the door sealed shut behind them.

"Fucking government film crew. They've been here ever since that goddamn Senator was here. They're filming all sorts of things for some bullshit propaganda movie they're planning on releasing."

"What kind of propaganda?" Mason couldn't help but wonder aloud.

"Same shit as always. 'Look at the deplorable conditions'. They wouldn't know deplorable from a hot bag full of dicks. I spent time in *real* prison. These biters have it good," Matty said, eyeing Mason closely. He had a hard glare, the kind earned in a place like this. "People don't get it. Biters aren't prisoners, they're merchandise in storage. All these labcoats should know that better than anyone, and yet they're in here helping all them documentary makers like Smiling Marcus. Cock munching liberals."

Matty swore their way to the cleaning closet where they broke out the hoses and supplies, including tall rubber wader boots. Mason rolled out the cleaning cart, feeling every bit like a maid at a hotel with all the brooms, blankets, towels, and soap bottles. They both sat down on folding chairs and started pulling on the waders.

"I don't get it," Matty said, looking Mason up and down. Aside from discarding his BDU top, Mason still wore only military issue clothing from his brown tee shirt to his black, polished boots.

"Get what?" Mason asked, grunting into one of his waders.

"Why you're here scraping shit with me. What did you do to wind up here?"

"I don't know," Mason said with a shrug.

"Like hell. Everyone here's done something wrong, pissed off the wrong guy, or is really a sick mother fucker that doesn't fit in with regulars."

"Which one are you?"

"Pissed off the wrong guy, of course."

"Sure," Mason said skeptically. "Are you sure you're not one of the sickos?"

"Fuck you," Matty sneered. "I'll tell you what landed me here. I kicked the shit out of an Admiral's son because he was drunk as fuck and trying to get on base with a whore. When I told him to go get a hotel, he told me he'd have me demoted. I told him to get the fuck out of here and he got out of his car and tried to pick a fight with me. So to calm him down, I zip tied his ass to a tree, but I forgot to set the parking brake on his Daddy's car, and it rolled into the lake. Thing was, Daddy was more pissed about the car, so I got the choice—come here or go back to jail. Same fucking difference, if you ask me. At least here I get to walk around more."

"Jail, huh?"

"Yeah, I made a few mistakes. What's your

story?"

"Nothing. I just got home from a tour in Egypt and drew a red card," Mason said. He didn't like lying, but he wasn't about to tell any part of the truth to anyone around here. If they knew why he'd been sent home in the first place, much less why he was here, they would zip tie him and shove him in a pen full of biters.

"Huh," Matty said, glaring at Mason.

Mason looked down and pulled on his other wader.

"You know everyone's saying you're a spy, that you're from the Inspector General's Office or some shit like that, come here to investigate us." He left the thought hanging. He continued to stare at Mason, trying to get a response.

Mason sat up and sighed, but said nothing.

"You don't deny it?"

"What's the point if *everyone's* saying it?"

"Point is I think it's a load of shit. The IG comes in on red fucking carpets. They don't send some burnt out veteran Ranger like you."

"Who says I'm burnt out?"

"I do. I can see it in your eyes, man. You drew the card because of something else. You're damaged goods, just like the rest of us. If you ask me, it's all just a big coincidence, on account of what happened on the Hill and that zombie half-breed they brought back from Midamerica with that Senator's kids. That bunch was here for a couple of days and stirred up all kinds of shit."

Mason shook his head. "I don't think I understood a thing you said."

"Don't you watch television?"

"I saw the news about the Hill, yeah," Mason said. Who hadn't seen it? It was on every day on every channel, even though no one said anything more than they were continuing their ongoing investigation. Drone videos were all over the Internet and news stations with experts telling viewers that *with this kind of devastation, we may never know the cause*.

"Yeah," Matty said, pulling on his second wader. "That Senator was here a few weeks back flapping his ass, collecting his sons—the ones who survived. He was giving speeches, looking the place over, talking with a bunch of lab-coats, like the bitch we just saw. Look, if you're really a spy, then you probably already know everything you need to know about her, but if you're not, watch out for her. That cunt's twat is more infectious than half of these biters and would eat you alive just the same."

"Jesus Christ, man," Mason breathed with disbelief.

"You're looking kind of pale, foreskin. I thought you were a Ranger." Matty stood abruptly and smiled down at Mason. "Push the cart," he said. "I'll hump the hoses."

Eight

Mason pushed the cart to the center of the line of cells, with Matty lugging four hoses ahead of him. The moaning had slackened a bit while they were changing, but now that they were in full view of the biters, the groans and desperate wails redoubled. Hands reached out between bars, sweeping at the air, hopeful for a scrap of food or warm skin to grab hold of.

"We keep them in pairs down here," Matty explained loudly, bellowing his words to make sure he could be heard over the moans and the chirping of one of the cart wheels. "Upstairs, they're all cut up so we keep them apart. We don't want them gnawing on one another. But down here, we pop a can of shut-the-fuck-up by tossing them into groups. Here's three, there they've got five. Those lab-coats said the biters complain less when they're in groups. I don't know where the fuck those stupid asses did their research, but they sure as shit never spent a night in here."

Matty stopped, his brow furrowed as he looked past Mason at a cell. "See what I mean? That's the cell they were looking at, right…am

I right?"

Mason looked at the cell Matty was pointing toward. Matty leaned side to side as he approached the cell, trying to look through the bars, moving sideways to get a better view. There were four biters in the cage, three standing against the bars, desperately reaching toward Matty, while one sat in the back on the bedding.

"Another weak-kneed son of a bitch. Those assholes were probably trying to film it to make us look bad. '*Look at this poor victim of consumption, wallowing in its own feces. Another example of the cruelty imposed by sanctioning.*' Cruelty, my ass."

"Are you going to help it out?"

"Why? That lab-coat that was up here, she knows about it. She brought them here specifically because of it, I'll bet you good money!"

"Yeah, but he looks sick," Mason said with only a hint of the concern he really felt. He didn't know what the protocol for handling a situation like this might be.

"If he was sick, he'd be whiter than that. He's got good color. Shit, he looks almost normal. Must be a Mexican."

Mason didn't have to ask about such a statement. Pigmentation was severely affected by the consumption pathogen, causing infected individuals' skin to appear bleached. This was because of a massive imbalance in their cholesterol levels, something that not only drove them to seek only meat for sustenance, but also impaired numerous other bodily functions, including pigmentation. For Caucasians the effect was near albinism. For Mexicans, Italians, Asians, Native Americans, and others with naturally darker complexion, their appearance was that of a fair-skinned Caucasian. For darker skinned individuals, the effect was either large, bleached patches or bright red hues.

"I don't think he's a Mexican," Mason said.

"Like you know shit. What have you been here, all of one day?"

"I just think that—"

"Stop thinking and push the goddamn cart."

Matty whistled the whole length of the cell block, even as they setup the hoses. He started stuffing orange plugs into his ears once everything was ready for work. Mason was already wearing his. Perhaps over time he'd get accustomed to the noise like Matty seemed to be, but so far it was a haunting drone that he couldn't ignore.

"Hand me a noose," Matty said, holding a hand out. Mason was carrying two nooses and sets of arm restraints. He gave half of his bundle to Matty.

"Now this is a little different than the second floor. All these mother fuckers aren't docile 'cause they're not under any meds. You hook them and lock them in, or they're gonna bite your ass, you got me?" Matty stared hard at Mason.

Mason nodded, trying to appear as sober as he could. It was more than a little distressing to think that he was about to go into the pens with biters. Upstairs, Matty had done all the corralling, showing Mason but not letting him near any of them because, as he put it, they were still contagious.

"This side's got the quarantines, that side's safe. You work them, and I'll take care of these mother fuckers. Don't try to be a hero. Just do it like I showed you upstairs."

"Got it," Mason said.

"Good. Go on and show me," Matty said with a wave.

The way Matty said it reminded Mason of his own father. *You think you've got that fast ball figured out? You think you can put that header on without busting a finger? You think you can save the world? Good. Go prove it.*

After two years overseas, Mason didn't think much about saving the world anymore. He had come to think that the world wasn't worth it. Not if everyone he tried to save wanted to stuff a knife in his back. These biters weren't much different in that regard.

Mason stepped up to the first cell and took a deep breath. In his training before coming here, he had fought with several zombies. They were much stronger than they appeared, mostly because when they did anything, they used *all* of their strength. They didn't temper their actions. As soon as he got the noose through the bars, he knew he was in for a fight. He drove the noose through and missed on his first attempt. The bars of the cell limited his range and he came up short.

"Jesus Christ, don't pussy foot around," Matty growled behind him. "One sweep or you'll be fighting a tug of war with *all* of them." Matty shot his hose into the faces of the three biters in the cell. The one Mason was struggling with let go of the noose pole and swept its hands over its own eyes. "Come on, weak dick," Matty said as way of encouragement.

Mason hooked the noose over the biter's head and hauled the thing forward, pressing its face into the cell bars.

"That's it," Matty told him. "Now use the restraint. Come on, you've got to be quick or he's gonna—" It was too late. As Mason fumbled with latching the restraint to the noose pole, the biter pushed off the cell bars and began yanking at the pole.

Matty shot water in their faces again as a second biter reached over to grab the pole.

Matty dropped the hose and grabbed the other end of the noose with one hand, nudging Mason aside. Matty was considerably bigger by bulk alone and easily tugged the biter back against the bars. With his other hand he latched a restraint bar to the noose pole and slid it toward the cell. It swung into place like flying down a zip line, clanking against the bars of the cell. Matty let go of the pole. The restraint bar only slid along the pole in one direction, so as Matty and Mason stood back. The noose pole flailed erratically as the zombie tried to pull free.

"Quicker next time," Matty said softly.

"Sorry," Mason said, disappointed with himself for failing.

"Did you think you were going to handle a pen of biters all alone on your first try or something?" He began laughing, picking up his hose and spraying the biters in the faces again. "Now get his arms restrained before he rips up the skin on his neck."

"Yes, sir," Mason replied evenly.

Nine

By the third cell, Mason was feeling more comfortable about subduing zombies. He still had to look at the restraint bar to latch it onto the pole, and he had trouble locking the captured biter's arms to the restraint bar using the harness, but he had captured seven on his own. Done with this cell, he pulled the noose loop off the biter and stepped back to collect the restraints he had tossed behind him. He retreated to the cart to get another bandage, spraying antiseptic over the cut on his forearm. Damned biter fingernails were thick and sharp. Matty hadn't warned him about that.

"Hey," Mason called out. "Do we ever clip their nails?"

"What?" Matty snapped irritably. "Does this look like a fucking salon?"

"Well, who shaves them?"

"They don't need to be shaved. They're all overproducing female hormones. Only one in ten grow beards, and hunters just kill those ones on sight most of the time. Too aggressive. Either that, or you have to castrate them like angry bulls."

Mason shivered at the thought.

"You don't even want to know about the children," Matty grumbled loud enough to be heard over the moans of discontent and hunger echoing through the cell block. Mason hadn't seen any children so far, but then again, the trade of underage infected was against federal law, so it stood to reason that none would be here.

Mason started lassoing a biter in the next cell to restrain it. His first batch of females. At first, he expected them to be easier, but their strength surprised him. The female grabbed the pole and nearly yanked Mason to the cell bars. Matty chuckled as he cut loose the group he had just finished. Matty had been keeping an eye on Mason's progress as he moved along at about twice the pace. He was already four cells ahead. Mason got the female under control and began to restrain her arms.

"You know," Matty shouted. "There was a guy who used to feel up the females after he caught them. Sick mother fucker. Don't let me catch you touching any of their titties or I'll report you."

Mason only nodded. That kind of debauchery made no sense to him. There were brothels in the Rurals that exclusively used zombies, but the only legal ones were in Nevada, and he thought it was more of a novelty than a real service. He hoped so, at least.

"Shit!" Matty yelled. Mason spun around to see Matty in front of the cell that the film crew had been interested in. "I need another noose!"

"What's happening?" Mason shouted back, moving toward Matty's position. Matty slid his security card over the keypad beside the cell. "What the hell are you doing?!"

The magnetic door buzzed, then clacked as it unlocked.

"Don't go in there," Mason shouted. "That's an order."

"I'm not losing another one," Matty growled.

Mason cursed under his breath and moved in on the female he had just captured. He needed the other noose pole to help out. He unhooked the rope on the outer end, and then slid forward to the restraining bar to pull the pins out and press the release. He yanked the two pins and had his hand over the release as the biter grabbed his arm. He fought against her strength to press the release latch. It gave with a loud snap and he shoved the pole into her face several times to break her hold of him. "Let go," he snarled, stepping back while hauling her arm to its full extent. With her arm wedged between the bars she was forced to let go and Mason grabbed the pole with both hands to free it from her neck.

"I need your pole," Matty shouted urgently.

Mason flipped the noose off the woman and yanked the pole free. He turned to assess the situation. The door to the cell was sliding open with Matty standing in front of it. Inside, the three biters were hovering over the body of the fourth, the one that had looked sick earlier. Mason knew he couldn't run faster than he could throw the pole so he hurled it and watched it slide across the ground toward Matty. Matty put a boot on it, reached down to grab it, and boldly strode into the cell before Mason had taken three strides.

Mason ran back to the other cell to grab another pole, but with the floor wet, he slipped while trying to stop. He fell, tumbling into the cleaning cart head first. He toppled the whole thing, spilling its contents across the floor. His hose began to spray into his face. He reached a hand down to block the water, realizing that the cart had fallen onto the nozzle and it was gushing water out of its broken side.

Mason pushed up to his feet again and clamored over the fallen cart. There was little he could do except watch as Matty swept a noose over the head of one of the biters. Mason snatched a pole and rushed forward, trying not to fall again.

"Hold this one," Matty bellowed as he locked the rope around one of the biters necks.

He wrenched the biter off the body and threw the pole like a spear. Mason dropped his pole and groped for the one coming at him through the cell bars. It swung upward due to the biter on the other end falling backwards once Matty let go. Mason jumped into the air and grabbed the pole. The pole lifted the biter by its neck. It flailed and kicked spasmodically.

"Shit," Mason hissed. He wasn't sure if hanging a biter would kill it or not so he eased and let the biter slump back down.

Matty looped a second biter and tugged it off as well, throwing the pole through the bars just as he had the first.

"Matty!" Mason reached a hand over to grab the second noose pole. "Matty!"

"Don't let go," Matty shouted, pointing a finger at Mason.

"Matty, get the fuck out of there, now," Mason shouted in as commanding a voice as he could muster. The two biters noosed at the end of the poles began to struggle, reaching and flailing at the noose rope around their neck and the pole itself. Their combined strength made it nearly impossible to control.

Matty kicked the third biter in the head, knocking it off the body of the other. He grabbed the biter by the hair on top of its head, lifting it up as though holding the severed head of Medusa so her eyes wouldn't turn him to stone. In a way, they were the same. The bite of a zombie was nearly as fatal. It looked like that had been the case for the fourth biter, laying face up in the back of the cell. Blood oozed from several gnarly wounds chewed into its flesh along its arms and neck.

"Curtis," Mason shouted, hoping that hearing his first name would ring some sense into him. "I can't hold two of them myself!"

"Grow some nads," Matty growled as he kicked the back of the knees of the biter he was holding, knocking it down again as it tried to stand. "Pull them back! I need to drag him out."

"What?!"

"I need another cell!"

Mason leaned back and pulled with all his strength. The noose poles slid outward through the bars of the prison cell, dragging the two biters with him. They still faced Matty, reaching and groping the air in a desperate attempt to grab hold of his warm, edible flesh. The moaning throughout the cell block had grown so loud Mason could hardly hear himself yelling "clear" to let Matty know there was room enough to get out. All the zombies were worked up into a frenzy like sharks smelling blood.

"Pull them back," Matty yelled.

"Fuck you, they are back! Watch yours, it's turning."

"Watch yours, he's trying to push off."

Mason swung the poles under his armpit and lifted his feet off the ground. The two zombies lurched into the air as though being hanged. Instead of groping toward Matty, they reached for the ropes digging into their necks.

"Go," Mason yelled.

Matty backed out of the cell, dragging the third biter by the hair. It flailed and beat at Matty's forearm with one hand while grabbing at Matty's hand with the other. Matty hit the biter's wrist with judo chops each time it latched on. Mason eased the other two biters down once Matty was clear of the cell door, but he still struggled to keep them under control. The noise and the smell of fresh blood smearing their upper lips drove them to savagery. The two shook violently. It took every ounce of Mason's strength to hang onto the poles.

Matty continued to back away toward the empty cells. There were two on the other side near where they had started the night so he was heading in that direction when he slipped. The ground was soaking wet from the gushing hose and with the upturned bottles of soap leaking out, the area had become slick. Matty fell hard, wrenching the zombie down with him.

Mason only caught a glimpse of the scene as he struggled with the two biters attached to the ends of his poles, but the one thing he saw clearly was Matty's hand letting go of the biter when they both struck the ground.

"Matty!"

Mason stared in horror for only a brief moment. The pole in his right hand jerked suddenly, throwing his arm up with it, enough so the pole smacked him in the face at full force. Mason's head snapped back reflexively as he swung the pole down again, turning his attention to the problem he had with these two biters. He needed to keep them inside the cell, but he couldn't reach the cell door without letting them go. He looked back to see Matty beneath the other biter, his forearm under the thing's chin and his other arm holding the back of its head. The biter had just as fierce a hold of Matty by the forearm and neck as it tried to pull itself down to his exposed flesh.

Fuck it, Mason thought, letting the two poles go. He started toward Matty, but felt helpless, like a man trying to outrun a bullet. The biter turned its head and sunk his teeth into Matty's forearm. Mason didn't stop. He screamed in anger and tackled the biter, hitting it across its back, clasping his arms around its shoulders, and taking it down head-first onto the slippery floor. Mason heard a scream from Matty just before the loud thwack of the biter's head cracking onto the smooth concrete. Mason slid to a stop before he pushed off the biter and stood in a hand-to-hand fighting crouch.

The biter began pushing itself up as well, but Mason kicked it in the face, knocking it onto its side. It hissed at him, baring human fangs soaked in red blood, both that of Matty's and its own. It glared at Mason with hateful rage.

Mason chanced a look behind him to where Matty was getting up, a hand over the bloodied wound on his other arm.

"Get to the main door," Mason yelled over the now thunderous echoes of moaning and wailing all around them. "Sound the alarm."

"I'm bit!"

"Fucking move, soldier," Mason shouted. He wasn't looking at Matty anymore. He stared down the biter in front of him as it stood and hissed. It took a step toward him. Mason dropped and swept its legs. It flailed and fell sideways, reaching forward as it did, desperately grabbing hold of Mason's closest arm. Mason stood abruptly, hauling the thing across the floor. It held on like a pendulum. He put his boot to the thing's throat and stood straighter to break the hold, but the biter simply grabbed his leg with its free hand. It felt like fighting an octopus.

Mason ripped the Velcro off his holster and drew his pistol. The memory his fingers triggered struck as hard as a bat to the chest. *Put down your weapon, soldier*, Mason heard himself in the recesses of his mind. *That's an order!* He shut his eyes in the hopes that he could wrest control over it, but it did no good. He couldn't forget his past, and the memory stunned him momentarily.

The biter's hands groping his leg helped keep him in the present situation. As hesitant as he was about using a gun again, he wasn't about to let himself get bitten. *Blam!* He shot the biter in the shoulder. Its arm fell limply to the ground. *Blam!* He shot it in the opposite leg. The biter only grudgingly recognized its own pain, beating on Mason's leg with its working arm. Mason stepped back to let it flail helplessly. He carefully moved across the slick floor toward where Matty was walking for the main door, head low, his back to the scene. Mason stopped, knelt down, took aim, and fired on one of the biters at the open door of the cell. *Blam!*

Matty looked back toward Mason, turning half way. He stopped and his eyes showed the despair and anguish of a dying man. Mason didn't move. He still knelt with his pistol drawn, aiming at the biter as it fell over its shot out-knee, toppling into a heap at the door of the open cell.

"You don't come back," Matty said, barely loud enough for Mason to hear.

"Keep moving," Mason ordered.

"I already feel it." Matty reached for his own gun, pulling it from his holster.

"Wait," Mason said, holding a hand up.

It was too late. Matty put the gun under his chin and pulled the trigger.

Blam!

Ten

"Fourteen months," Warden Mitchell shouted.

Mason wasn't sure if he couldn't hear the warden because he was still in shock, or if the deafening noise of the cell block earlier that night had caused permanent hearing loss.

"We've gone fourteen months without so much as a sniffle. No accidents! No nothing! A perfect record until you come along and in two days—*two days*—you've been here two days, and you kill one biter, put two biters into intensive care, and—" Warden Mitchell stared at Mason with a fatigued look of resignation. His voice lowered to a near whisper, and yet Mason could still hear him.

It must be shock, Mason thought.

"I don't even know what to say about Matty. Do you have any idea how bad this looks?"

Mason said nothing.

"At ease, soldier," Warden Mitchell finally breathed, his ire seemingly spent.

Mason realized he was still standing rigidly, still holding his salute.

"This again?" the warden asked, waving a half salute toward Mason. Mason lowered his own salute and stood at ease.

The warden sank into his plush leather chair and lit a cigarette. "Want one?" he asked.

Mason shook his head.

The warden took a drag on his cigarette and let the smoke out slowly as he rubbed his temples. "Well, this is going to be one fucked up day. Why couldn't you have just left the fucking biters in the cage?" he asked, almost pleading.

"I didn't open the pen, sir," Mason replied.

Warden Mitchell glared at him, taking another drag from the cigarette, exhaling hard toward Mason. "You could have said something or done something, dipshit. Why didn't you shoot that fucking biter trying to eat Matty? You're some kind of marksman, you know that? I wouldn't have believed it if I hadn't seen the goddamned video. Bam – right in the knee, from twenty feet away! Dead-on perfect hit. Couldn't you have done that to the other biter's head before it bit Matty?"

"The in-processing training videos clearly indicate that lethal force is to be—"

"I know what the fuck the videos say," the warden shouted. He took another drag from his cigarette to calm himself. "I'd rather be chewing you out over killing a few biters than having to write a letter home to Curtis' family.

Plagued 59

Next time, fucking shoot to kill, do you understand?"

"Is that an order, sir?"

"You're goddamned right it is. Only there better not be a fucking next time. I've already got enough scrutiny and congressional oversight to handle. That shit on the Hill made sure of that. And that's another thing, Jones. How the fuck am I supposed to trust you? I can't put you back in there to work alone, and I can't put anyone with you because…." The warden threw his hands in the air and waved them at Mason. "You're just fucked," he said while inhaling from the cigarette again.

"I can handle working alone, sir."

Warden Mitchell raised an eye, breathing out smoke from another drag. The cigarette was almost done. He held it next to his mouth and turned in his chair to look out the window at the morning gray. Another dismal dawn on the island. "Fourteen months gone to hell," he said softly, taking one last drag as he spun in his chair to mash the cigarette out in his ashtray. "With all those reporters all stirred up over the incident at the Hill, this is worse than the last time."

Accident Report of September 3rd regarding Little, James, Corporal, US Army, assigned to Rock Island as night shift patrol specialist. Official records indicate he was overcome while attempting to corral and *detain two non-infectious inmates. Unofficially, he was found with his pants around his ankles in a cell that previously contained two female inmates, both of whom were freely roaming the cell block after having partially eaten Corporal Little's exposed neck, arms, and legs. Both female subjects were without clothing and one was still partially restrained at the arms.*

"No one works alone on graves," Warden Mitchell said at last. "I'll rearrange some other men's schedules. In the meantime, consider yourself relieved of duty."

"Sir?"

"Take the day off, but don't leave the island. And for fuck's sake, stay away from any reporters if they find you."

"Sir, should I check in tonight?"

"Just a phone call is sufficient. Call your duty officer at your normal check-in."

"Yes, sir," Mason replied.

"Unless there's anything else, you're dismissed," Warden Mitchell said, waving another half intended salute toward Mason.

Mason retreated to the door and left the warden's office. Outside were four desks for the administrative team, all empty. Another door led to the reception desk where Mason heard a man's raised voice.

"…I've been sitting here fifteen minutes," the man was complaining loudly. Mason stepped into the reception area and halted. The Sergeant behind the desk looked up at Mason imploringly, expecting the warden. The large man in front of the counter crossed his arms and huffed.

"Are you in charge here?" the man asked.

Mason shook his head, looking the civilian up and down. It was easy to tell the hunters from everyone else on Biter's Island. After seeing them for a few days, Mason knew the tell-tale signs: the rough and calloused looking hands, the leathery skin of long exposure to the outdoors, the loose, aged t-shirts that rip easily if grabbed hold of, the boots—the kind Matty wore—not military attire, but for the handling of zombies, probably a grade above.

"Well then, what idiot *is* in charge around here?"

"That would be me, Mr. Opland," Warden Mitchell said from behind Mason.

Mason stepped aside while turning. The warden had snuck up on him too easily. Mason's senses were still dulled.

"Hank," the large man snapped. "Just Hank."

Opland, Henry, aka "Hank", 53 years old. Recent survivor of Biter's Hill disaster and eight-year licensed zombie hunter. He was the fifth person to apply for a license and maintained the record for longest tenure in the trade, all four of his predecessors having died or turned. He and the other survivors from the Biter's Hill incident had been airlifted to Rock Island for quarantine. All except one survivor was released from quarantine. Of the released survivors, only Hank Opland remained to continue zombie trade activities.

Mason stiffened.

Eleven

Mason waited outside of the warden's offices out of view, hiding under the canopy of a large tree near the street. Hank came out fuming, swearing audibly as he stomped to the sidewalk. Mason waited until Hank turned east toward the civilian compound before following him. With the sun just rising, there was a great deal of activity. Soldiers of every branch were crossing the streets from the barracks and heading for the mess hall. Weaving through them, Mason took on a certain level of anonymity that allowed him to follow Hank without being noticed, even when the big man stopped to look back, glaring toward the prison complex and uttering more oaths before continuing for the gate house.

A long chain-link fence with a crown of barbed wire spanned the width of the island, separating the civilian population from the military personnel. At both roads there was a guardhouse that served as a checkpoint to limit the hunters, slavers, and vacationers from having unfettered access to the military facilities. Hank stopped at the gatehouse to show his identity, then walked briskly toward the golf course.

They were still on the road when Mason began jogging to catch up to Hank.

"Sir," Mason called.

Hank stopped and waited for Mason, sizing him up with his eyes. Hank was a much bigger man, a lot like Matty in a way.

"Mr. Opland, can I have a word with you?"

"It's Hank. Did your boss forget to get my phone number while he was screwing me?"

"Sir?" Mason asked in confusion.

"What do you want, boy?"

"I overheard you talking to the warden," Mason said. "About Biter's Hill."

"What about it?"

"Were you one of the survivors?"

"What's it to you?"

"The dead biter from this morning's incident. Was it one of yours?"

"You're goddamned right he was," Hank snapped. His eyes narrowed and he thrust a finger toward Mason, poking the air between them as he hissed the words, "And he wasn't just some biter, kid." His sneer lingered even as he turned around and started walking away again.

Mason kept up with the bigger man's pace, walking two strides to his side just in case Hank got angry. "Sir, there was nothing we could do for it."

Hank stopped and turned, his face red with rage. "He had a goddamned name! The one that's dead—Mike—he was with us in Midamerica. He got bit saving us." Hank sucked in a deep breath. Mason saw a twitch under the big man's eye. "They said they would try to cure him, but it didn't work," Hank went on, throwing his hands in the air with the same contempt carried in his tone. "First it was something about the inhibitors he received being different, then they said it was because he was too fresh, that the antidote didn't work on him because he was so new!"

"I'm sorry," Mason said.

"Yeah, like hell you are."

"Hey, I lost a man trying to save your friend," Mason replied hotly.

Hank's features softened, but he still appeared irritated.

"Did the warden tell you what happened?" Mason went on.

"Not much. He said three of my stock were involved in an accident and had to be disposed of."

"Disposed of?"

"Put down. Their injuries were bad enough to affect their resale value, so they're compensating me at the going market rate."

Mason stared through Hank as the words settled in. He had been lied to before. There was nothing unusual about that in the Army or in politics or the world as a whole. *For God and country*. That was the biggest lie of them all. Standing on a wall facing a horde of the living in Egypt or the dead here didn't make a difference when it came to that. Both were about appearances. The appearance of stability and control in an environment far from it. The only difference between Egypt and Biter's Island was that they could control what people saw here. In Egypt, it had been a free-for-all.

"I'd like to tell you what happened last night, but I can't without running the risk of you going off to the warden or the reporters or others who might open their mouths to the wrong person. It would all get back to me, I can assure you."

"Why's that?" Hank asked, squinting with one eye suspiciously.

"Because I'm the only one alive who was there when it happened."

"Well, I can keep secrets pretty well. Mike's been in quarantine for four weeks and up until five minutes ago, only the warden and that bitch chief scientist Kennedy knew who he was."

"Kennedy?" Mason asked with interest.

Twelve

"Is this him?" the Senator asked as he took a seat behind the desk. The encounter was weeks old, but Mason remembered it clearly. The location of the meeting was a back room at *Blanc*, one of a dozen restaurants in Larimer Square. Mason had been driven in from the airport in a black SUV with tinted windows. His driver may as well have been a mute for as much as he talked during the forty-minute drive. Mason looked out the window and kept track of the markers, wondering where everything was and where he was going. After what seemed an endless barrage of traffic signals, the driver pulled into an alley and parked the vehicle. They went in through the back door, past the cooks and kitchen staff, who acted as though they hadn't noticed either of them arrive, then straight into an office with no windows. When they arrived, the office was occupied by a man in an expensive white suit.

"You're here," the man had said, putting down his pen and stuffing his notepad into a drawer before getting up and walking past Mason, smiling at him but saying nothing else.

Mason had thought to follow the white-suited man, but the silent driver put a hand on Mason's shoulder and pointed at the visitor's chair. When the Senator arrived, Mason stood, his mind racing, wondering why a Senator wanted to see him, and why here, in secret?

The driver nodded to the Senator.

"Jones?" the Senator asked.

"Yes, sir?" Mason replied.

"Go get me a Bourbon, would you?" the Senator asked Mason's silent driver. They were alone then. The Senator walked past Mason, grinning ear to ear. He sat down and waved for Mason to do the same. "Do you know why you're here, Lieutenant?"

"No, sir."

"Do you know where you are?"

"Downtown Denver, Colorado."

"Specifically? I'm told you have an eye."

"Your driver took the 70 after Peña from the airport, to the 36 to the 70 again, where we passed through two checkpoints, then to the 25 south, exiting Fox Street and travelling past the ballpark, taking Blake Street to 14th Street before coming up a back alley to this restaurant."

"Shit, you *are* good. It's a damned shame. I could use someone like you in my office. Do you know who I am?"

Mason didn't answer right away. He still didn't know what all this was about.

"William Jefferson," the Senator told him. Mason remained still.

"You don't follow politics much, do you, son?"

Again Mason said nothing. Senator Jefferson wasn't someone he would vote for.

"All right, I get it," the Senator said. "If I was in your seat I probably wouldn't want a bunch of idle chit-chat, either. I have a proposition for you. How would you like to do something great for your country?"

Mason didn't get a chance to answer. A knock came at the door followed by the silent driver carrying a tall glass with ice and Bourbon in it.

"Do you have the file?" Senator Jefferson asked the driver as he accepted the glass. The driver nodded. The Senator waved a finger toward Mason as he sipped at his drink. The driver removed an envelope from the inside pocket of his jacket, revealing the butt of a 9mm pistol Mason already knew was strapped to his belt. The driver tossed the envelope past the Senator onto the top of the desk in front of Mason. Mason eyed the driver as he stepped behind the Senator with his hands crossed in front of his belly, ready to draw down if there was trouble.

Mason looked at the envelope but didn't touch it.

"Go on, soldier. Take a look."

"I don't understand," Mason replied.

"Look, son, the zombie plague has had its way with us long enough. I'm a patriot, just like you. I want to put a stop to it. Really, I do," the Senator said with what sounded like sincere concern even as he took another sip of Bourbon. Mason wasn't sure if he should buy it, though. Just because the Senator said it well didn't mean he meant anything. "I want to make America great again. I want to put a stop to all the animosity toward us around the world. I want to clean up America and tear down the walls that divide this great nation. District Rules, Rural Rules, and then there's the Plagued States where there are no rules, and yet it's all America. We're supposed to be *one* nation under God. I haven't seen our union for over ten years. The America I grew up in is the America I want your children growing up in, but we've got to start by fixing it today."

"I don't have any children," Mason replied flatly.

"It's a figure of speech, son," the Senator said with a disarming smile.

"It was a good speech, sir."

The Senator took a drink and set down the glass, turning to look over his shoulder at his man. "I thought you said he would be on board."

"He passed all the psych profiles," the driver said calmly.

"He did?" the Senator asked skeptically. He turned and looked at Mason. "Do you understand what kind of honor this is to be chosen for a mission like this?"

"I don't understand, sir. What mission?"

"Hasn't he been briefed?" the Senator snapped at the driver, turning to glare at him.

"No, sir," the driver said. "We did show you his file. He's the one we took from the psych ward."

"Oh, yeah," the Senator said, snapping a finger, then spun in his chair to look at Mason again, measuring him, gauging him as he took another sip of Bourbon. "Does his file say anything about his attitude?"

"A few reports of insubordination since the incident, but otherwise a match."

"A few huh?" the Senator said. "Let me ask you one question, Jones. When you used to stand the wall in Egypt and you could see those screaming protestors marching up the street with their picket signs and their sacks full of rocks, how did it feel knowing you weren't allowed to shoot them unless they breached the wall? Even when they hurled stones and Molotov cocktails at you? Even when their snipers fired at you from nearby buildings every other day? Or their bombs exploded from cars charging the check points? How did it feel to be holding in your hand the weapon that could put a stop to it—your M-14—but guys like me sitting here at home told you to stand down instead of engage? Did that piss you off?"

"Which of those questions did you want me to answer, sir?" Mason replied.

"Fuck this," Senator Jefferson said, throwing his hands up as he stood. "He's not the one."

"Maybe," the driver said with a shrug. "Maybe not."

"Why are we wasting our time with him? Find me someone else. Someone who gives a shit."

"Sir," Mason tried to interrupt.

"Shut up, son. You fucking blew it. It was nice knowing you, kid," the Senator said while scooping up his glass. The Senator stopped at the doorway, his back to Mason and the driver. Mason didn't stand. His driver didn't budge. The envelope remained on the desk in front of him.

"Sir?" the driver asked the Senator after a short silence.

"Send him in anyway. Maybe she can change his mind."

"Yes, sir," the driver said blandly. The Senator closed the door behind him as he left.

"What was this all about?" Mason asked the driver.

"You're due at Fort Hood in the morning for in-processing and training. We have you on a red-eye. Take the envelope. It has some background about the facility and people assigned. Commit what you can to memory by the time we reach the airport. I've got your travel orders in the car. Your contact at final destination will be Danielle Kennedy. Can you remember that?"

"What is it that you guys want me to do? Where am I going?"

"Right now, you're going to the airport. Kennedy will brief you on your assignment once you get to your final destination. It's probably better for you to just go along for the ride. Get the lay of the land. Keep your eyes and ears open."

"I don't understand," Mason said, staring at the envelope. "You know why they took me off the wall in Egypt, don't you? You know why I'm back home, right?"

"Yeah, I do. That's kind of the point."

Thirteen

Mason had no intelligence information on Doctor Danielle Kennedy. Aside from seeing her briefly in the cell block the night before, he had no idea where he would even look for her. Hearing Hank say her name gave him hope that maybe he could find a way off this miserable island sooner than his tour would end. He suspected they would stop-loss him into another two years on the island if he didn't at least make contact with her. That's the kind of corner he was being backed into. They probably even tipped off the warden, if he wasn't in on the whole thing. Why else would he ride his ass like he was? But that only raised a bigger question: what did the warden have to be afraid of?

"You want another beer?" Hank asked as he stood up from the booth in the small tavern next to the Meat Market. "I'm gonna take a leak and get another round for myself."

"Sure," Mason replied, brooding over the half-empty bottle he was milking. It was getting warm.

"Let's take 'em with us," Hank suggested.

"I need to set up for the day."

Mason walked beside Hank as they wove through the lot full of vehicles the hunters used for collecting their merchandise. Every vehicle was raised higher than what seemed practical, mobile platforms with bars and rails that could be used to repel an assault from the ground. Chains and cables secured all manner of tool, weapon, and supply that wasn't welded or bolted to the vehicle. Each truck was unique in some way, as though each had been built in a junkyard by lunatics who believed the world was coming to an end. The vehicle they stopped at made all the rest seem like cookie-cutter copies by comparison.

"What the hell is this?" Mason asked Hank as the big man began climbing a metal ladder affixed to the back of the craft.

"It's a duck," Hank replied, sounding offended by Mason's tone. "An amphibious vehicle. I know it don't look like much, but it saved our asses at the Hill."

"Are you telling me this thing floats?"

"Mostly. It rides pretty low when the gas tanks are full, but otherwise she'll power across the channel."

"And you hunt in this thing?" Mason asked, tugging at the ladder to make sure it was sturdy before climbing up after Hank.

"Don't be an idiot. Nobody hunts in their truck. You do it on foot."

Mason reached the top and stood on a flat deck ringed by waist-high railings. The center half of the vehicle was under a canopy supported by a row of cells made of sheet metal with only narrow slits that allowed air flow and some light in, but no more than a finger could get through otherwise. All the cells were the same except the last one closest to the cockpit. It was a larger open cage made of vertical bars on all four sides with a locking cage door and a bunk bed.

"The luxury suite?" Mason asked jokingly as he peered into the last cell.

"Peske used to keep Kitty in there."

"Who kept what?"

"This was Peske's rig back on the Hill. When the shit hit the fan, he drove us all to safety. All the way to Midamerica. That's where the rescue choppers came for us, so we left the duck there. After they let us out of quarantine, I hired on with another group of hunters, traded them my catch for a ride. I got the duck and I'm back in business."

"What about Peske?"

"He's dead. He had a heart attack just when we were getting saved."

"So was this cat of his some kind of lion?"

"Kitty?" Hank guffawed. "She was his half-breed."

"Half-breed?"

"Half woman, half zombie," Hank said,

and the thought of it struck Mason as hard as a bullet. "Partly cured. Non-infectious. Some kind of experiment they did on her early on when they were working on the cure. Like a feral cat, that girl, but she was Peske's draw. She kept people coming to his pens first. He was the number one dealer on the Hill because of her."

Mason thought of the notes about the research facility here on the island, beneath the prison. He hadn't been inside it yet, but he knew there were cells inside the lab. Cells meant to hold and control up to ten test subjects. Nothing in the notes said any test subjects had ever escaped, though. And he knew nothing about the events at Biter's Hill except what was on television, which was very little.

"So what happened to her?"

"You know, you ask a lot of questions, kid. Why don't you start answering some of mine, like what happened to Mike?"

"I think they cured him, after all," Mason replied, took a deep breath, and recounted everything that had happened the night before, omitting their encounter with Doctor Kennedy. He didn't think that would help him at the moment, and it might have incited Hank more than anything.

"Huh," Hank said when Mason was finished. "Well, that settles it, then. Thanks for telling me."

"Settles what?"

"I'm getting the fuck off the Island, that's what. I've got one body left, thanks to you, so I'm going to go sell him to another trader and head for the Bend in the morning. I've got a bad feeling about this place."

"You and me both," Mason said. "Can you do me a favor?"

"Depends on the favor."

"Can you get me in contact with Doctor Kennedy?"

"How about I give you her phone number and you call her yourself. I don't trust that bitch, and the last thing I want is her knowing you and me talked. You got me, kid?"

Fourteen

Mason woke to his alarm clock buzzing, the red LED glow showing 6:00 PM. He put on his uniform and left for his meeting with Kennedy. As he walked toward the Meat Market, several flatbed trucks passed him going the opposite direction. They were hauling caged biters to the prison for the night. Civilians left the market going in one of three directions: the parking lot, the hotel casino, or the same tavern Mason had been in with Hank that very morning. Mason followed two hunters into the tavern and found an empty booth near the back next to the pool tables. A group of hunters were playing a game, glaring at him suspiciously, eyeing him with an almost malicious intent. Mason took off his uniform top so that only his tight brown t-shirt covered his upper body. He flexed his hard muscles and glared back at them. Mason may not have been as big as Matty, but his arms and chest had the solid look of a prize fighter. It was enough to get his point across. The hunters didn't bother him as he sat waiting for Kennedy to arrive.

When she showed, she strode in proudly on

a pair of high heel shoes, with her lab coat over her shoulder. She sauntered toward the bar in a tight black skirt and even tighter red top. She turned heads looking like that.

"Set me up the usual, Mac," she announced. "What's the special? I'm stuck working all night again."

An amber liquid spilled over cubes of ice in a short glass and was placed on the bar in front of her. She took it and turned around to face the room, planting her elbows behind her, her eyes scanning the room from one end to the other. The way she was standing, Mason saw the square outline of her smartphone zipped up in a pocket against her hip. The bartender was telling her what they had on special to eat. She took a slow sip from the glass as she listened. When her eyes reached Mason's corner of the room, she smiled and turned to the bartender.

"The Cobb. Send it over there, will you, Mac? I see an old friend."

"Sure thing, Danni."

She boldly strode toward Mason, her lips curling upward in a sassy smirk.

"I thought I recognized you," she said as she stopped in front of his table. "Jones, right?"

"Yes, ma'am."

"What are you having?"

"Nothing yet," Mason replied.

She looked over her shoulder toward the bar, throwing a hand up to catch the bartender's attention. "Get me a beer for my friend," she called out. The bartender nodded and she turned her attention back to Mason, smiling. "Mind if I join you?"

"Not at all," Mason said, sliding out of the booth to stand. His courtesy made her smile.

She was a tall woman, his own height in her heels. She slid into the bench seat opposite him and put her drink down out of the way, tossing her lab coat onto the seat beside her. Mason sat down again, settling one arm on the table, turning his shoulder toward the hunters who were now all watching him with veiled interest.

"Ignore them," she said. "Tell me, Mason Jones, are you in or out?"

"I don't know what I'd be in if I answered that question."

"Hmm," she said thoughtfully, taking a deep breath and sighing before saying, "So are you really stupid pretending to be smart, or really smart pretending to be stupid?"

"How about a little ignorant pretending to be both."

"All right, I think I can work with that." She smiled again, tapping her glass with a finger as she considered his stoicism. "I was told you are particularly observant, that you don't miss anything. Some kind of photographic memory?"

"Eidetic memory," Mason told her. "I was

diagnosed with it in high school. Why does everyone keep asking me about it?"

"It's useful for this…let's say, position. You are hyper-observant, which sets you apart. It's one of the things that got you into Benning."

"Yeah, well, after five years Army, I think being a truck driver like my guidance counselor suggested might have been a smarter move."

She held an accommodating smile, the kind that showed her ire. "You're good at insubordination, Jones. You pissed off Jefferson, and you're pissing me off, too. He told me your fate was in my hands, so, unless you like this hell-hole, how about you try making some productive conversation."

"Yes, ma'am," Jones said evenly.

She didn't seem satisfied with his response. She continued to glare at him, picking up her drink again to take a sip. "So tell me what you know."

"I was hoping you could clue me in on what I *should* know. I got taken out of the hospital, put on a plane, driven to a restaurant in the Districts in Denver—and I don't even have a District Pass—met with a Senator who wants to save America by stopping zombies—as if that's possible—given an envelope with thirty pages of intelligence on this facility that I was told to commit to memory, given your name to contact, and then they put me into two weeks of training for zombie hand-to-hand and close quarters combat before shipping me here to scrub cells on the graveyard shift. That's the sum total of my last two weeks."

"Nobody told you what we're doing here?"

"All I know is there's a research lab below the prison."

"You've seen the rest of the island, I presume. I mean, you have eyes, don't you?"

Mason nodded, but instead of answering, he sat up straight, not taking his eyes off hers as the bartender put a beer down in front of him. She smiled, saying, "Thanks, Mac. Where's the salad?"

"It's coming, it's coming," the bartender said over his shoulder as he retreated.

"Do you come here often?" Mason asked. She laughed heartily. For as much as he thought he should hate her, he was having trouble putting the description others had painted of her to the woman sitting across from him.

"All right, I'll let that one pass," she said with a demure smile. "Unless you're trying to come on to me."

"No, I just figure you know the bartender," Mason shrugged.

"Yeah, well, sometimes you need a little help forgetting what you've seen, you know?" She held up her glass to him. He held up his beer and they touched the two in a toast before taking a drink.

Mason had no trouble agreeing with her, thinking of his own past and what he wished he could forget, but drinking never helped. It only emboldened the memories. He shook off such thoughts and took a deep breath. "So what is it I'm getting into?"

She gauged him a second, not pressing him on what he'd said. "I want to test your eyes. Can you tell me what kind of tattoo those two men playing pool have without looking?"

"The one with black hair and a beard doesn't have any tattoos," Mason said. "The other one, the guy thin as rails, has sleeves of tats covering both arms. I only really made out a skull on his left arm and a lot of fire on the right. You, on the other hand, have a dove on your right ankle."

"You noticed?" she asked with a wry smile, raising her eyebrows. "What else about me did you notice?"

"Does this count as productive? I mean, this place is a real hell-hole, like you said."

"Humor me," she went on, still smiling.

Mason considered a moment before opening his mouth. Was she leading him just to disarm him, to worm her way through his defenses? He still couldn't trust her. For as long as they had been sitting together, she had yet to say anything substantive.

"You don't have a badge or wallet anywhere on you, not even the pockets of your lab coat."

"You can see in my coat?" she asked in surprise, looking at herself.

"When you put it down. The pockets, I can see them from here," Mason said while pointing.

"Oh, well, that's good. For a second I thought maybe you could see down my shirt too," she said and laughed.

Mason smiled and picked up his beer to have another sip. "Your phone has a pink frame," he told her. "The one in the pocket of your skirt."

"How the hell did you see that?" she asked, looking down at her lap.

"Last night. You were carrying it in your hand."

"Damn, you *are* observant."

Mason shrugged and took another sip of his beer. She unzipped her pocket and withdrew her pink phone. "You don't see many of these on the island," she said while swiping the screen to login. "Signals are jammed over here, at least the public band. This one, though," she said, shaking it for emphasis. "This one is on a private frequency. Do you know why I'm allowed to have this?"

Mason shook his head.

"Because I'm in charge," she said. "Can

you work with that?"

"I don't see why not."

"Great, then why don't you tell me why you're here tonight?"

"Your salad," Mason said, leaning back in his seat. She shot him a questioning glare for a split second. The bartender stepped up next to the table and put a salad down in front of her. She began to laugh again, an intoxicatingly real, hearty laugh that worried Mason. This was all a game to her.

"Get me another, would you, Mac?" she asked the retreating bartender, pointing at her glass as she raised it to take another sip. "So why are you here?" she asked Mason.

"I was assigned."

"No, here, tonight. You called me. This number. That means you want in. If you didn't want to play ball, you would have just served your six months and gone home like the others."

"Others?"

"Oh, do you think you're the only person we've assigned here?"

"I still don't understand."

"You don't mind if I eat, do you?" she asked. She took a bite of salad and looked as if she were lost in thought a moment as she chewed. "Answers. All right. Well, before last night's brilliant zombie killing of yours, we wanted your help in closing this place down once and for all."

"Close it down?"

"In the military, you'd say it's no longer of strategic importance."

"But close it?"

"Look, don't you think America has had enough of the zombie plague?" she asked.

Mason had heard nearly those exact words from the Senator's mouth. It made him feel like he was listening to talking points. The difference between hearing it from her as opposed to Senator Jefferson was that he was beginning to like the sound of *her* voice.

"What can you do about it?"

"Well, cure it, of course."

"How? It would take twenty years to round them all up."

"This isn't the time to get into a discussion about logistics, Lieutenant," she said, taking another bite of her salad. She turned her head to chew, watching him from the corner of her eyes. "You can help us put a stop to the zombie infection once and for all. Entire *states* can be restored. Think of all the jobs and the livelihoods that would affect. The biggest land rush since Oklahoma. Over three states restored, with new cities built by new investors creating new jobs and stimulating our economy to bring us back on top where we belong. Your own home state is a split-state, right? Ohio?"

Mason nodded, sipping his beer.

She took another bite of her salad to let her words sink in. As much as Mason would have liked to believe it didn't mean anything to him, he was, after only two days, sick as hell of this place and willing to listen.

"We can't restore the union the way things are. This place, this continuation of the slave trade—*of slaves*, lieutenant. They're using innocent people as *slaves*—all because they cling to a way of life that was thrust upon them by accident. I can fix it. I can put an end to the consumption pathogen, but not if these drunk, tattooed, inbred, retards playing pool on a remote island in the worst hellhole on planet Earth continue to exist. As long as they keep bringing in more slaves, businesses won't put a stop to their acquisitions. Did you know it's cheaper to manufacture trucks in America now than it is in Mexico? The Chinese care more about the CAC, FTSE, and DAX than they do the NASDAQ or NYSE. As a nation, we're becoming a second-world economy.

"This virus has ruined America, and I'm sick of it."

Kennedy stabbed her salad and took another bite, chewing slowly and watching Mason closely.

"It's only my second day and I'm pretty damned sick of it too," Mason said and took another sip of beer.

"Well, then, what's it going to be?" she asked.

"What do you need me to do?" Mason asked. She smirked, stabbing her salad again to take another bite.

Fifteen

Memories only haunted Mason when he closed his eyes. They used to invade his waking thoughts too, whenever he slowed down enough that his mind had time to travel wherever it wanted. And it always went to the same place: Egypt.

The rattling of the RPG going off along the wall hardly shook him. In his dream, it flew across the street as haphazardly as a butterfly, bouncing and weaving on unseen eddies and currents, leaving behind a contrail of white smoke. No hiss or high-pitch whistle. Even the explosion pounded with an eerie quiet. The only sound was the familiar *whit-dit-dit* of an M-14 rifle as it burst clusters of rounds down over the crowd.

Put down your weapon, soldier, Mason shouted over the gunfire. *That's an order!* The young soldier, hardly more than a boy, lifted his eye from his M-14 and turned his head to see Mason aiming at him. How many times had Mason already told him to cease fire? *There was a fierceness in the young man's eyes*, Mason would later report to his superior officer, but that didn't describe the wild fury that had taken utter control of Corporal Smith. The Egyptian mob beneath the wall scattered, receding like startled rats. Smith ignored Mason once again, pulling the trigger to fire another burst of rounds at the crowd. Mason held one hand on another soldier's wounded arm in an effort to staunch the gushing blood, leaning his weight on the wound. *Soldier,* Mason shouted again. Smith turned to glare at Mason again as he switched magazines. *Don't do it*, Mason heard himself pleading. *Screw you*, Smith snarled as he turned the M-14 on Mason, shooting a stream of bullets.

Buzz, buzz, buzz. He heard the bullets whip by his head. *Buzz, buzz, buzz.*

"Wake up, asshole!" Lieutenant Thompson groaned.

Mason jerked, suddenly wide awake. He slapped the alarm clock. He could hear himself breathing hard even though he knew his heart hardly took a beat.

"Sorry," Mason said, rubbing his eyes.

"Why'd I get stuck with someone on graves?" his roommate moaned and covered his head with his pillow.

Mason stared at the dark floor beneath his feet and tried to wrench the memory from his thoughts, but it was like cement. He could still see the accident report clearly.

Smith, William A., Corporal, 2nd Ranger

Battalion, 75th Regiment, assigned to U.S. Embassy Defensive Controls duty after completion of Ranger training. Became a father two months after deployment. Killed three and wounded sixteen Egyptian civilians during a protest march on the U.S. Embassy after a rocket propelled grenade was fired from the crowd that wounded two soldiers. When ordered to cease fire, he refused, and eventually turned his weapon on himself.

That was the official report, the one he had signed. Sometimes he regretted that as much as killing the poor kid.

Mason used the hall phone to punch in the extension of the duty officer and waited for an answer. He stood in the darkness of the bay of rooms, alone under the dim light of the exit sign posted above the door.

"What do you need me to do?" he had asked Kennedy. She hadn't given him an answer, at least not a good one. She smiled and finished her drink before telling him she would be in touch, that she had to talk it over with the Senator, and that he should just keep doing what he was doing.

"What *am* I doing?" Mason asked.

"Blending in," she had told him.

"Phillips," the night duty officer said as he picked up the other line.

"Sir, this is Lieutenant Jones. The warden—"

"Oh, yeah, he called me a few hours ago," Sergeant Phillips interrupted. He sounded agitated, like he had been dreading this phone call since he heard the news. "Look, we still need you to come in, if you're feeling up to it."

"That's fine," Mason replied. "I'm not tired anyway. I'll put in my shift."

"Oh, good. Good. That's the Ranger spirit. I'll see you as soon as you get here."

Mason dressed and went to the prison complex in a fog of thought. He hardly noticed the blacklight glow to the cement walls of the man-trap gate. Mason waved at the soldier peering down at him from atop the gate tower as he made his way to the side door of the complex. Unlike during the day shift, it was so quiet at night it felt like death hovered over the island.

There was no one in the munitions room when Mason arrived. He swiped his card and punched a code to open one of the inventory control doors that showed a pistol and belt holster through the glass. The door unlocked and Mason withdrew the weapon, checked it for rounds in the chamber, and then tested the trigger. It was in working order. Ammunition and clips were openly available. Mason took a loaded clip and slid it into the butt of the gun. Fifteen rounds should be enough for any contingency, but after his first night, he wished they issued high-capacity magazines.

"Ah, Jones," Sergeant Phillips said when Mason knocked on his open door. Phillips sat rubbing his temples when Mason first saw him, staring at his computer screen. He stood and saluted as Mason entered the room.

Mason returned the salute.

"Have a seat," he offered. "How are you getting along?"

"Fine, sir," Mason said as he settled into the square, wooden framed chair.

"I'm sorry to have to call you in like this, but we're running below MPO tonight without you and Matty."

Minimal Personnel Occupancy, or MPO, for Rock Island Prison Defense Facility consisted of two roof guards, two tower guards, and six patrol guards who doubled at station post details. Technically, that made Mason part of the prison defense guard even though his primary job was janitorial services.

"Can't afford any point reductions right now, given the circumstances," Phillips said and looked up behind Mason.

Mason turned at hearing someone entering.

"Ah, Chavez, you know Lieutenant Jones, I trust?"

Sergeant Chavez leaned against the door frame with a cup of coffee in one hand and his hat in the other. He nodded toward Mason.

"Evening, sir," Chavez said with a bleary smile.

Plagued

Mason nodded and smiled back. "How did you get roped into this?" Mason asked.

"I was volunteered," Chavez replied. "You ready?" he asked, nodding his head as if to say *let's go*.

They made their way down to the second floor where it looked like a slaughterhouse again in the operating room. Brown blood stains smeared the floor everywhere, bits of smashed flesh ringed the ground beneath the head of the operating table, and lines of dried blood meandered like streams toward the drains. The biters in the cells moaned hollowly, as though they were confused instead of desperate. It was quieter than down in the main cell block, their chorus didn't excite one another as it would normally.

"I vote we leave the ones in the cells alone and just—" Chavez said, waving a hand toward the operating table with a look of disgust. He poured his coffee onto the floor. "I don't even know what to say about that."

Sixteen

Mason sat on the folding chair in the janitor closet pulling on the waders. He and Chavez had hosed down and cleaned the operating table and floors around it, but left the biters in their cages as Chavez had suggested. Mason wasn't too concerned with doing a good job in light of the circumstances. And besides that, he had been told to *blend in*. Chavez sat down next to him, yawning widely.

"I hope they get a replacement for Matty in a hurry," Chavez said. "I don't want to get stuck on this duty again…no offense."

"None taken," Mason replied. "What do you mean again? You've had to do this before?"

"I'm one of the four alternates. Last time there was an accident I was on this assignment for a month!"

"Well, I can do it alone if—"

"No one works alone on the floor," Chavez said.

Mason stood up and took the four hoses off the wall. "Well then, let's go clean up. Do you want to push the cart or lug the hoses?"

"I'm fine looking like housecleaning. Go plug in the hoses," he said with another yawn and wave toward the door.

Mason carried the hoses out to the bibs and dropped them. Even the roar of hundreds of moaning biters hardly registered as he knelt down to attach the hoses. He thought it strange that he was beginning to ignore them as though they were just background noise. Even with his earplugs in, he could still make out the squeaking of the cart wheels over their drone.

"I'll catch, you clean the first five, then we switch," Chavez suggested. "It goes faster that way."

"Matty had me catching my own, then cleaning."

"I'm sure he did, but Matty was an asshole. Catching and cleaning yourself takes forever. Matty liked taking his time. It meant he could be down here longer. Personally, I hate it in here."

Blend in.

Chavez started catching the zombies in the first cell as Mason added the spray nozzles to the hose and got out the cleaning solvents.

"So why do we have to clean them at night like this?" Mason asked. It bothered him since he arrived, but he had never asked Matty. He hardly had the chance to get a word in edgewise with Matty. "Why not clean the cells by day when they're at the Meat Market?"

"They do. They clean them the minute the damned things are taken out, but there are two kinds of biters in here, you know. Those bastards there," he said, pointing the noose toward the line of cells Mason had worked the night before, the ones that had been operated on and had been through recovery—the ones for sale. "Those ones are taken out every day. The only shit in there is what they've done since coming back and getting fed. These ones, though," Chavez said, turning with the noose and driving it through the bars of a cage, catching one of the zombies. He grabbed the thing with expert precision, just like Matty. No chasing the thing or missing, or having to try twice. Just a sweep and the loop was over the back of its head, and a second later he was hauling it to the front of the cell, pinning it as he swung the restrainer down the pole where it clanged into place against the cell bars. Chavez pointed at the biter he had captured and wagged a finger at it. "These sons of bitches have been in here all goddamned day, sleeping and crapping at their leisure."

Chavez grabbed the next noose off the cart.

"We can skip that group tonight," Chavez added, pointing at the sterilized biters. "Let the day crew deal with it. You can't tell the difference half the time anyway."

Half-assed work, Mason thought, but didn't say anything. Mason was beginning to get the impression Chavez was one of the lazy ones he would have had to keep an eye on in his command over in Egypt. He wondered if Chavez was like that in Egypt too, if maybe the reason his team was compromised in an ambush was his fault. Maybe that's why he was here. Everyone on the island that he'd met so far had something in their past that earned them some kind of punishment. Mason wondered if he was actually an inmate being deceived into thinking he was free. It would make sense, in a horribly sinister kind of way.

"There you go," Chavez said to the second biter, patting its head after checking the restraint. "Gentle as a kitten," he added, and the zombie thrashed. "Whoa!" Chavez laughed, stepping back. "That one's hungry. Let me double check the restraint before you go in there."

Chavez kept his distance as he tugged on the wrist straps binding the biter to the cell bars. It shook again and its moan became more of a growl, deep like a lion.

"No, he's good. It's all yours."

Mason didn't move right away. He stared at the two zombies restrained against the cell bars, their faces wedged against them, their pale skin pulled tight, their hazy eyes wide with rage. It reminded him of the soldier in Egypt, the one he had shot. The eyes were what haunted him, so absent of reason, so filled with malice. Mason couldn't fathom what would drive someone to such an extreme.

Chavez picked up a noose from the cart and stepped up next to Mason.

"Don't worry, man," he said. "I've never had an accident and I've been here years."

"Well you know my record, don't you?" Mason said, looking at him sidelong.

Chavez laughed and slapped Mason on the shoulder. "You want me to do it, pussy?"

"No, I've got it," Mason told him and walked up to the cell door card reader. He swiped his card and heard the buzzing. The moaning throughout the cell block redoubled, the Pavlovian response to the sound of freedom or feeding, or something Mason hadn't yet figured out. A door was a door to these things and it could have meant all of that and none of it. Mason stuffed his card into his cargo pocket as he pulled the cell door open.

Mason began hosing out the feces on the ground, dragging the hose all the way into the cell so he could spray at it and push it along the cinderblock wall. Normal prisons had beds and plumbing and a toilet, but not here. The pallet was six feet long by six feet wide and had a pile of blankets that the zombies somehow turned into a nest-like roost. Mason put down the hose and dragged out the blankets to replace them.

Chavez had noosed the first of three biters in the next cell and was coming back for another noose pole and restraining bar. Mason threw the old blankets to the ground and grabbed three new folded ones from the cart.

"You know, you can just leave the bedding too," Chavez said as he followed Mason to the cell door. The aggressive biter snarled and shook at his restraints again and Chavez stopped, letting Mason walk through the cell alone. "We're not the Hilton," Chavez said and started for the other cell.

Mason turned his back on Chavez. Doing the job right didn't take that much more effort. As his father would have said, it takes more effort avoiding work. It made Chavez's laziness even more irritating.

There was a sudden and loud clank behind him. Mason tensed, nearly jumping in fright. Then he took a deep breath and said "funny" over his shoulder as he turned, expecting to see Chavez laughing and asking something like "jittery?" as he dragged a noose pole along a cell bar, clanking it once just for effect.

Mason's heart clenched tight like a fist. A gaunt face stared at him, plump eyes bulging with need. The noose stretched the loose skin around its neck toward the pole raking through the cell bars as the zombie lurched one more step closer. Mason's surprise and disbelief shed at the sight of the unlatched restraint. It still trapped one of the zombie's arms against its chest, latched to the turned pole. The other arm was free.

The blankets in Mason's arms fell to the ground. The hand latched onto Mason's shoulder. Mason threw his left arm in the air to knock it free, but the biter's cold, boney fingers held as though stitched to his shirt. Mason reached his other hand for his pistol too late. The biter took one more step and pulled at Mason. Decaying breath moaned over him, a soupy blend of rotten fish and curdled milk assailing Mason through its bared teeth that seemed determined to find flesh. Mason tried to step back but his foot caught on the lip of the bed pallet.

The zombie pushed forward and they both plummeted to the pallet. Mason wedged his arms between them a split second before striking the ground. The impact jarred his senses. The zombie's body sagged over Mason with the unwieldiness of an enormous sack of flour. The zombie's head gave a hollow whack against Mason's forehead before bouncing off. Mason's arms were the only thing keeping its teeth at bay. He drove the zombie up to elbow's length, leaving it perched above him, dripping its saliva and hissing.

Mason turned his head. The biter let go of Mason's shoulder and instead grabbed the back of his neck, pulling itself closer. With the zombie's weight over him he couldn't reach his pistol. Mason kicked his legs to turn his lower body sideways.

"Help!" Mason yelled between his struggling grunts.

The zombie pitched slightly to Mason's left. Mason's forearm slipped across its chest. In a second it would slide off him, he realized. He extended his forearm to help it along, rolling to his right and pushing the thing away. It fell on its side, its hand still hooked to Mason's neck.

"Hang on a second," Mason thought he heard Chavez calling, his tone one of annoyance.

Mason started to roll. The biter's hand slid from Mason's neck. Mason pushed against the biter's chest with his left arm to lift himself free. The biter grabbed his wrist with its other hand. Instead of turning and rolling away from the biter, it yanked Mason back like a dog on the end of a leash.

The bite landed square on Mason's upper arm, digging into the exposed flesh of the bicep.

"No!" he screamed and rolled toward the zombie to keep it from ripping the flesh with its teeth. The pain seared the length of his arm. With his other arm he grabbed the thing by the back of its head and pulled it closer, jamming its face into his arm, driving its nose flat. He knew he couldn't wrench the thing off without tearing loose a hole in his arm. He knew that it wouldn't be able to bite through if he could push against its mouth. He also knew he wanted to kill the thing by ripping its head off and beating the skull on the ground until he, himself, died.

He'd been bitten.

He pulled harder, crushing the biter's head in a hug as he continued to roll over on top of it. He felt the teeth gnashing the muscle and bone of his arm and the pain shot through him like bullets.

Mason let go of the head once his weight was over it and he hastily reached for his pistol. The biter tried to thrash free. The sudden tearing in Mason's arm caused him to cry out in pain. The biter's eyes were still wide with rage as it began to reach a hand to Mason's neck. Whether it meant to push him off or pull him closer, it didn't matter. The rage was still within those eyes, the rage of a man no longer capable of rational behavior, no longer able to think beyond wild necessity. Mason stuffed the barrel of his pistol into the eye socket of the biter.

In Egypt, Lieutenant Mason Jones closed his eyes when he pulled the trigger on his fellow soldier. He had already taken aim. He already knew where the bullet would strike. There was no need to watch the young man die.

"Go to hell," Mason snarled as he stared wide-eyed with hate at his victim now. *Blam!*

Seventeen

Mason felt the jaw slacken against his arm. His weight sank over the zombie as it went completely limp beneath him. Its arm thumped onto the pallet. When the pistol went off, blood burst out the back of the biter's head like a water balloon hitting the ground. Small bits of brain and skin and bone lay randomly scattered around the exit wound. Its remaining eye slowly lost its fierceness as the eyelid sagged with the rest of its body.

"What the fuck?" Chavez shouted from the cell door. "What the fuck happened? Are you all right, man?"

Mason turned his shoulder to pry his arm free of the teeth. He pushed the jaw open wider to slip his skin out of the dead biter's top teeth. Pain erupted again like a red hot coal being pushed through his skin. He let out another cry of pain as blood oozed out of the wound and into the biter's open mouth.

"Holy shit," Chavez said as he knelt down next to Mason. "Hold on, man, I'll call for help." In a second Chavez was gone.

Mason slid the rest of his wounded arm out

of the biter's mouth and rolled onto his back, dropping his pistol onto his chest. He put a hand over the wound and felt the sting of it over the slick heat. He felt light headed, not from the wound so much as the adrenaline and the sudden realization that he was a dead man.

No wonder Matty pulled the trigger.

He picked up the pistol off his chest and sat up. He looked at the biter sprawled out on the pallet beside him and aimed the pistol at its head again. *Blam!*

The biter's head knocked sideways as another bullet ripped through it.

Mason fell backwards over the dead biter, leaning his head on the biter's chest. *Keep your head elevated to prevent going into shock*, he told himself. He brought his knees up and used one to take aim on the other biter in the cell. *Blam! Blam!* Two rounds struck the back of its head, splattering blood and gore onto the wall and out onto the floor in front of the cell. The biter sagged in its restraints, but didn't fall. Mason wanted to kill more of them. He aimed at one of the contained biters across the cell block. It leaned against its bars, arms reaching desperately toward the bloody dead. It could smell the fresh kill, but its wild eyes were empty of understanding. It hungered. Mason hungered too, for revenge.

He dropped the pistol onto his stomach. He was already one of them. The anguishing thought hovered over him, pressing on his chest. He struggled to breathe, to control his anger. The pain in his arm reminded him where he was. He put his hand over the wound to staunch the blood loss.

Chavez ran into view, sliding to a halt in front of the open door, staring wide-eyed at the two dead biters and Mason.

"Someone's on the way," Chavez said. "I called for medevac."

"Inhibitors," Mason groaned. The pain on his arm was still like fire, pulsing with each beat of his heart.

"They'll bring them," Chavez said.

"Get the first aid kit. I need a compress and bandages."

"On it," Chavez said and started to leave. He stopped suddenly and came into the cell to kneel beside Mason. "Look, I'm—" He shook his head. "I can't let you keep this," he said, taking Mason's pistol. Mason reached toward Chavez, but he was already standing and stepping back. "I'm sorry, man."

Mason didn't have the strength left in him to fight Chavez over it, nor did he think it mattered. Matty had killed himself thinking there was no way out. Mason had other ideas. They cured Mike. Maybe if they got to him fast enough they could cure him before he turned.

Chavez was quick in coming back, kneeling beside Mason with the first aid kit.

Mason took three compresses and held them over the wound. The sting was worse than any wound he had ever sustained before, although this was probably the worst trauma he had ever had, too. Chavez rolled a bandage around his arm as tight as he could. Mason sucked in a hiss of pain, but Chavez didn't stop.

The buzzing of the door and the redoubling of the moaning all around them announced someone had arrived. Chavez hastily taped the bandage.

"Hang on," Chavez said and went to the cell door. He stopped and held out a hand to wave as he looked down the cell block. "Are you *alone*?" Chavez yelled in anger.

"I'm on patrol," another voice called back defensively. "I was on sub-floor two when I got the call."

"Where's the medic?"

"It's fucking two in the morning," the voice replied irritably. The voice had a body that came into view of the cell, a soldier wearing black body armor. He looked in at Mason and assessed the dead biters. "Holy fucking shit," the soldier said. "What the hell happened?"

"We need the lab medic on duty," Chavez said.

"It's two in the morning. Ain't nobody *in* the lab!"

"There's always someone in the lab. Go

down there and get them!"

"I don't have access," the soldier complained.

"I'll go. You stay here with him. Don't let him have a gun."

"Did he do this?" the soldier asked Chavez. "Did you do all this shit?" he asked Mason, pointing between the two biters. Mason nodded wearily. "Yeah, your gun privileges need to be revoked, man."

"Cut the shit, Johnson. He's been bit," Chavez growled, which sobered the soldier and made him step back from the cell bars. Chavez looked in on Mason. "I'll be right back. They're just downstairs."

Mason nodded, but didn't think anyone was down there. Why would they be? It was two in the morning, just like Johnson said. Chavez ran off anyway and Mason listened as the door hissed and clacked and the moaning all around them rose in volume again.

Johnson didn't say anything once they were alone. He stood outside the cell, worriedly looking in at Mason from time to time, looking both ways up and down the cell block nervously the rest of the time. Now that Mason had a tight bandage over the wound, the fiery sting gave way to dull throbbing that pushed small needles of pain up and down his arm with each pulse of his heart. Mason imagined small shards of glass being forced through his veins. That would have been tolerable except that the fire of it left him numb where it had already torn through. He couldn't feel part of his arm anymore and that concerned him.

Mason didn't like waiting. It was the military way, but in the line of fire or when a man was down, soldiers always took action. It was part of their training. Mason sat up abruptly. His heart rate was normal. He had avoided going into shock. His blood loss was controlled. He should have gone with Chavez.

"Hey, man," Johnson said, holding a hand up. "You should just chill out."

Mason moved his hurt arm with his other hand, lifting it gingerly to get it out of the way so he could stand up. The moment it moved, though, the pain flared up again. He sucked in his breath through clenched teeth, closing his eyes to wait out the pain. His heart pounded harder and it felt as though he could hear each beat. He dug the foam plugs out of his ears and threw them to the ground, hoping the moaning around him would help drown out the sound. Hearing his own heart like that made him think he was too close to death.

Mason tried to stand. Blood rushed to his head and it felt as though he were on a ship tipped sideways. He kept thinking to correct himself by leaning, but each time he did it seemed the boat switched angles and he had to correct himself again.

"You're looking really pale, man," Johnson told him from outside the cell. "Just sit back down before you fall down, OK?"

Mason started to agree with Johnson when he saw black spots filling the ring of his vision. He fell back to a sitting position and tried to control the blackness. It wasn't shock. He knew that much. This meant he was about to faint. He took deep breaths to counter the effects, ignoring the pain clawing its way down his forearm toward his hand.

Why was it in his forearm, he wondered, looking down at his arm. His vision was hazed over with blackness, leaving only the center of his vision unaffected, and even that seemed to have trouble focusing. He watched his hand clench against the pain. He could feel his fingers and wrist moving, but not his elbow.

The stairwell door clacked and hissed again, and Mason was relieved by the rising volume of moans in the cell block. Chavez and a woman wearing a white lab coat arrived and both stopped at the entrance to the cell. The woman was a thin redhead in her forties with deep worry lines, and he hoped they were her normal appearance.

"We've got to get him downstairs," she said.

"Come on, Jones," Chavez said, moving into the cell. "I'll help you."

"No, I can't," Mason replied, shaking his head. He was still seeing black spots dot his vision at the edges. "I'll faint. I tried standing."

"You're way too big for me to carry you," Chavez admitted.

"Blankets," Mason said, feeling breathless from his controlled breathing. "Noose poles. Stretcher."

"Good idea," Chavez said with a smile. "Johnson, get two of those nooses off the cart!"

"Doc," Mason said. She gingerly stepped over a pool of blood left by the biter's head wounds and knelt down beside him. "Doc, my arm is going numb."

"Do you feel that?" she asked.

He nodded.

She began walking her fingers up his arm. "Tell me when you stop feeling it."

"There," Mason said.

She stopped and made a quick slicing motion across his arm, scratching his skin with her nails, enough to make a welt. Mason didn't feel it, but instinctively pulled his arm away. The pain of doing so shot through him and he groaned in agony. "What the hell did you do that for?"

"I thought you said you couldn't feel anything," she told him.

"I didn't."

"Did you feel me cut you?"

"No!"

"Good. We'll use that mark to see how fast the pathogen is neutralizing your nervous system."

"One field stretcher," Chavez said proudly as he came into the cell with Johnson behind him. "Let's get you downstairs."

Eighteen

Mason held his arm tight against his chest as they carried him into the lab. They passed through a large steel door and into a hallway with plate glass on both sides. To the left were offices overlooking the hall. To the right was the laboratory.

The doctor swiped her card and the door to the lab opened. She held it to let Johnson and Chavez carry Mason through.

"I ain't never seen this place, and I don't never want to again," Johnson was saying as they lugged Mason through.

The lab was an enormous open room with two surgical tables. Rolling medical equipment was scattered throughout. A countertop with cabinets above and below ran the length of the far wall. A row of eight cells took up the wall nearest the door. Mason glanced at them as they carried him to the center of the room.

"Put him down here," the doctor said. "Get him off the blanket. I need to make a call." The doctor went to the far wall and picked up a telephone to punch in an extension. They eased Mason onto the surgical bed.

"Come on, Jones, turn a little," Chavez said. Mason was hardly paying attention to him. The cells weren't empty. Every other cell had an occupant, four in all. Two were strapped to beds with ventilators and other devices keeping them sedated and alive. A bearded man and a woman occupied the other two cells. The man paced back and forth in his cell like a caged lion, his eyes glaring at Mason and the others. The woman, on the other hand, sat on the bed in the back of her cell with arms wrapped around her legs, a blanket over her shoulders. The light in the laboratory was bright enough to reflect off their eyes, and in both of them he saw the milky haze he had become accustomed to seeing in all zombies.

A half-breed.

Both Hank and Matty used that word to describe the woman that came back from Midamerica. Mason wondered if this was that woman, but if so, who was the bearded one? Another half-breed, for sure. Maybe they experimented on them here. Maybe they made them. Or maybe that was what he'd become.

Mason tried to sit up.

"Whoa, whoa, whoa," Chavez said, putting an arm on Mason to keep him down. "Doc!"

The doctor turned with the phone at her ear. "I'll call you right back," she said and hung up. She hurried to the table and stepped in front of Mason, who was now sitting up with Chavez holding his good arm to keep him from falling.

"Jones, I need you to listen to me," the doctor said. "We're going to administer the curative, but it has to be dosed against the level of toxicity in your blood."

"Them?" Mason asked, pointing at the cells. He could hardly think of how to form a sentence or say what he was feeling. Crippling pain gripped his hand, and now he felt the sensation of fire in his shoulder. He squeezed his pained hand, trying to smash away the ache.

"They're *special* test subjects," she said. "We use them to incubate the cure."

Mason looked at her.

"Now lay down on your side so I can work on that arm."

Mason reluctantly slid back onto the table with Chavez's help. They helped him on his side, lifting a padded plate so he could lean against it as she could work on his hurt arm. The doctor instructed Chavez to put restraints across him and around his wounded arm to keep him from moving. They restrained his other arm and legs as well.

"Just so you're aware, Lieutenant, I'm going to clean and dress your wound as best I can. We're not going to give you anything for the pain or put you out. We need you lucid when we administer the curative, but I don't want that arm getting banged around or hurt any worse than it already is. The only good side effect of being bitten by an infected subject is that your pain receptors in the area are all dulled to the point you won't feel a thing.

"I'm also going to put this weird looking helmet on your head and this bite guard in your mouth. The bite guard has holes so you can breathe through it even with your teeth gnashed, so just bite down on it and keep it like that. I know it all sounds strange, but you'll thank me for it later."

She slid the helmet over his head and clicked the chin strap on, then held out the bite guard.

"Open up," she said and placed the guard over his upper teeth. He bit down on it and sighed. "Let me get a tray setup," the doctor said and went toward the long counter, opening drawers and cupboards to collect things.

"Hang in there. Don't worry," Chavez told Mason to assuage his fears.

Mason wondered if his concern was that obvious in his eyes.

"The cure works. I've seen it before."

Chavez patted him on the shoulder, but Mason hardly felt it. *Seen it before?* How did Chavez know something like that when no one else did, and how had he seen it before if he hadn't been down here with someone who needed it? Suddenly, Mason didn't trust Chavez *or* this doctor. He tugged at his restraints, but they were solid. He was trapped.

And that wasn't even the worst of it. The pain he felt in his shoulder was climbing up his neck, causing his hands and feet to tremble. His arms and legs came next, involuntary spasms jolting him against the restraints.

"Hey, doc," Chavez called. "He's hitting stage one!"

"Already?" she asked, looking his way.

Mason's convulsions hit harder suddenly, and although he could hear Chavez and the doctor arguing, he couldn't make out what they were saying. The light intensified, washing out everything, leaving behind what seemed like the inside of a cloud, obscuring sound and sight and everything else. He felt cold, as though he was naked and outdoors in the winter. His skin burned from the chill.

The world around him grew foreign, absent of time and substance in his fog of consciousness. The here and now faded to memories swimming near and far, some ringing him in a wide arc, hinting at their existence, but not coming close enough to be recognized, while others rushed him in a frenzy. Memories with bites, razor sharp teeth like ravenous sharks, savagely striking and pulling away, each coming from different angles and without warning. He started to recall Christmas when he was eight, the year his father bought him his first pistol—no, that was his fourteenth Christmas, when he was having sex with his girlfriend before leaving for Egypt, and the fight on the tennis courts with that bully Tim Hadowick in fourth grade. By the time he realized none of them were the same memory, he couldn't remember what the first had been at all. He just remembered Tim Hadowick standing over him and laughing, calling him a pussy, and him wondering what that word even meant.

He hated grade school. Clumsy, uncoordinated, un-liked, and poor. He hated his father for putting him through hell, moving them from city to city, never settling down. Construction. Mason hated construction, but didn't know why. He was just certain he hated it, and it had something to do with his father, the son of a bitch.

And then there were the eyes. They watched him through the fog of his thoughts, waiting for their moment to strike, and he feared them like no other. Whatever memory they represented, he knew them to be the most painful he had ever endured, and yet they waited, lurking, watching him, and biding their time.

Mason took a deep breath. His body shook violently, uncontrollably. He was screaming and he didn't know why. The doctor stood next to Chavez, both several feet back, both staring at him with grave concern. Behind them the two half-breeds watched as well, the woman from beneath her blanket, which she now wore tightly over her head, her hands cupped over her ears. The male glared with unabashed interest as he held the bars with both hands, his head pressed between.

"Fuck me," Johnson said from where he stood against the glass near the door. "Can I go? This is freaking me the fuck out."

"Yeah, get going," Chavez said. Johnson didn't hesitate. He swiped his badge, fumbled for the door handle, pulled it open, and rushed to get through and into the hall. He may as well have been running, and Mason wished he could be with him, free of this place. What other tortures did they have in mind for him?

"Lieutenant, are you all right?" the doctor asked.

Mason nodded.

"Well, before you have another spell, I'm going to get that arm sewn up."

She pushed a chair and a tray next to him and picked up a pair of scissors as she slid a mask over her mouth and nose. She was wearing protective goggles already. Mason watched her cut off the bandage on his arm. He felt the tug of it when she pulled it away, but his arm was otherwise numb. It interested him a little to finally understand why the zombies had no fear of injury. Even though he watched her squirt water into the holes left by the bite, something that should have ignited unbridled pain, he felt nothing.

This was what it meant to be a zombie.

Nineteen

His second set of seizures ended just as abruptly as they had started. Memories of the world spun inside his head and left him with vague recollections of things he had done and seen in his life, but confused him as he recovered. Piecing together the remnants of his thoughts made no sense, as though he were stitching the wrong fabrics together. And like waking from a dream, the notions of what had been swimming in his head vanished as the world around him came into horrific focus.

"Hello, Jones," Kennedy said. She was sitting in the chair in front of him, a mask over her nose and mouth, broad safety glasses over her eyes, and a sanitary hat over her head.

"Huh," was all Mason could say through the bite guard.

"So what do you think *now* about our little zombie problem?"

"Huh," Mason said, not sure what she meant at first. He knew she was being sarcastic, but not entirely certain how it reflected on him. He struggled to remember how he knew her and when he had seen her

Plagued

last, and it irritated him that he was having trouble with recalling something he should know.

"Good, I'm glad we cleared that up," she said, slapping her thighs as she stood up.

Where was the other doctor? Mason looked around the room and finally saw her almost behind him. She was sitting at the counter with her back to him, working on some kind of blood testing device. It relieved him to know he wasn't alone with Kennedy. Mason remembered the other doctor's conversation—a one-sided conversation, at that. "Doctor Kennedy? Sorry we got cut off earlier. No, we have the cameras rolling. Everything is setup. He's past stage one now. About ten minutes ago. Yes, ma'am. I'm ready now. Oh, you're still on the mainland. But it'll take you fifteen minutes to get through…no….yes, ma'am, but waiting for stage two…no, ma'am…yes ma'am. You're the boss." She had hung up and slapped her hands on her lap angrily, then turned to smile at Mason. "Don't worry," she had said.

Mason was worried.

Doctor Kennedy pulled on a pair of latex gloves and moved the chair out of the way. She took out a flashlight and held it to Mason's eyes. He flinched and she put her thumb on his eyelid to lift it.

"You're in stage three of degradation right

now, Jones," she told him. "When the next wave hits, you're going to suffer some more memory loss and you'll feel disoriented coming out, but it should be the last stage you'll undergo before reversal. The curative I've developed must be administered on waking subjects because it causes vomiting which could kill you if you're sedated, so I'm sorry you have to go through all this. The nice thing is now you can tell off any mother on the planet when she says you don't know the meaning of pain. Child birth has nothing on this."

Kennedy swabbed Mason's shoulder above the bite wound. He couldn't feel it, though.

"Are you ready, Wendy?"

"Yes, ma'am," the other doctor said, carrying a loaded syringe on a tray over to Doctor Kennedy. Kennedy picked it up and jabbed Mason's arm with it in one motion and without a word. Mason watched her squeeze the plunger evenly until she emptied the amber liquid into his arm.

"Congratulations, Jones," Kennedy said as she put the syringe back on the tray. "You're cured."

"Huh," Mason replied unenthusiastically.

"We'll consider that productive conversation," Kennedy said and Mason could see she was smiling by the way her eyes tightened and her cheeks and ears raised behind her mask. Mason wondered if he should know what she was talking about. It was some kind of inside joke, but he hardly remembered her, much less the joke. *More* memory loss, she had just said. *More!* How much memory loss had he already suffered?

Tingling ran up and down his arm. He stared at it, wondering if the pain would return with it. Would the memories return as well?

"Wendy, let's get a local ready for this arm," Kennedy said as she lifted the dressing and peeled back the tape holding the bandage to his skin. She gave Mason a pat on the forearm and walked away.

The male half-breed continued to glare at Mason through the bars of his cell. Chavez sat on a stool at the bench, an arm on the counter, looking bored. Mason wondered why he was still there. He had a paper cup of coffee beside him, so at some point he had gone and come back.

"I'll want to do a comparison of his blood with the half-breed's as soon as he's stable," Kennedy said to the other doctor. "Rudy, do you mind assisting?"

"Not at all, ma'am," Chavez replied through a yawn.

Mason groaned as the tingling in his arm became that lick of fire again. A jolt like lightning struck him suddenly, seizing him so that his whole body went rigid, and in that moment, it seemed as though his skin was being torn from him, that his bones were breaking, that his muscles were flexing so fiercely that they were tearing themselves from their anchors. He let out a wail and closed his tearing eyes.

In the darkness, he only saw eyes, hundreds and hundreds of eyes glaring at him. He recognized those eyes, the haunting of a hundred restless nights and wandering-minded days, the soldier in Egypt. The one he had been forced to kill. The eyes struck him like serpents, biting him with teeth like stilettos that injected the poison of remorse and doubt. It was endless, strike after strike hitting him randomly throughout his body. If the burning that engulfed him was an inferno, then these bites were the lashes of the devil himself. Mason's torment hardly waned except between lashes when he had time to breathe hard and fast through his nose and frothing mouth.

He felt a tremendous tug on his chin and heard a woman's voice shouting spit it out over and over again. The bile in his stomach burned his lips and for a moment of lucidity, he realized what was happening. He opened his mouth and spit the bite guard away, heaving up what felt like his own entrails.

Again, the lashes came, and he seized against the eruptions of pain, for how long he had no idea. They came in waves, each one only mildly more tolerable, which in his state, he attributed only to a dulling of his senses as a whole.

When it subsided enough that he realized it was fading, he opened his eyes, hoping that the ones that haunted him in his dreams and memories—those of the very devil himself—were gone.

Kennedy sat in a chair only a few feet away, staring at him with clinical fascination. All he could see were her eyes, how they lacked compassion, how they resembled the eyes of his nightmare. He closed his eyes in an effort to recognize what had tortured him and could only see her eyes glaring at him from the recesses of his mind. Tears fell freely as his lips and jaw trembled with the need to cry.

"You handled that well," she said softly. "I think the worst is behind us."

Mason opened his eyes only to see the same dark pupils that haunted him from his past staring at him now. Egypt. She was Egypt. How could that be?

"Wendy, get a rinse bottle for his mouth and a new bite guard, and clean all this up, please. I've got to go see the warden. You two can handle things, I assume?"

"Yes, ma'am," the other doctor said.

"Blood draw," Kennedy said while snapping her fingers. "I want it in ten minutes.

Text me your findings." Kennedy took off her mask and goggles and tossed them into a waste can near the door. She swiped her card and stepped into the hallway before tapping the screen of her pink framed phone. She held it to her ear as she looked in through the glass at Mason, her eyes as sterile as her demeanor. Mason wondered what she was thinking. She looked lost in thought. Yes, her lips said. She looked down as she turned to leave. Halfway down the hall, she looked at him again and waved. It reminded Mason of the kind of nonchalant gesture two friends parting after sitting for coffee might give, and it was as phony as all hell. The one memory he did still have echoed in his head. He heard someone telling him, "I don't trust that bitch." And neither did Mason.

The other doctor rinsed his mouth with a water bottle and told him to spit it out, not to drink it. He was so thirsty, but he did as she said. She wiped the vomit from the table with a towel and let it all fall to the floor. She used the same towel with her feet to push it out of the way.

"Let's get you on your back," she said as she unhooked the strap around his left forearm. She let it fall away and Mason sighed while watching Chavez pick up a noose pole off the wall beside the fire extinguisher. The male half-breed slid to the back of his cell, his eyes never leaving Mason. He didn't need to see Chavez or the pole. He must have known the routine.

The doctor unlatched Mason's chest as well and he began to roll easily onto his own back, more thankful for the change of position than anything else.

"You're going to have to slide toward me a little," she said. Mason used his good shoulder to lift and slide himself closer to her. She eased the restraint at his chest again and removed the restraint around his right arm completely. "I'm going to need this arm," she said, guiding it under her armpit as she sat down on the chair next to him. "Just relax." She pulled a tray closer to him and took a rubber strap from it.

"This one is being uncooperative," Chavez said jokingly. "Can I use a Taser on him?"

"No," the doctor snapped.

Chavez drove the pole through the bars, extending it all the way. Mason turned his head to watch so as to avoid seeing the doctor draw his blood. He hated needles. As Chavez fished for the half-breed, it moved side to side, dodging the sweeps. Suddenly, the half-breed lunged forward and caught the pole, pulling it with a vicious tug. Chavez's arm stretched straight and he fell forward. The half-breed pulled the pole hand over hand, stepping close to the bars as he reeled Chavez in, his right wrist wrapped in the catching rope.

"Shit," Mason groaned as he tried to sit up.

"I haven't even stuck you," the doctor said. She put a hand on his chest to keep him down.

"Doc," Mason wheezed in alarm.

Chavez's arm was hauled between the bars and the half-breed jumped forward, turning it at the elbow to pin him as his other arm reached out to the back of Chavez's head.

"Doc!" Chavez managed to yell just before the half-breed slammed his head into the bars. Chavez was stunned by the blow and his head wobbled when the half-breed released him. The doctor spun in her chair, saying, "Oh my God!"

Mason's eyes widened at the sight of the half-breed's actions. It pulled Chavez's left arm into the air and pinned it against the cell as well, sliding it up and down over and over until there came a chirp and a sudden clack of the lock releasing. The half-breed pushed its cage door open and heaved on Chavez's pinned right arm once more. Chavez yelled in pain as the bone cracked. The half-breed let Chavez go and Chavez used his left hand to reach for his pistol. He managed to rip open the holster and have the pistol out before the half-breed was jumping onto him. They spun and the pistol flung across the room, sliding toward the wall with the plate glass windows.

Mason began unlatching his restraints. The doctor was running across the room for the phone. The female half-breed leapt against the bar with hysteria. The restraints couldn't be removed quickly enough for Mason, especially in his groggy and weary state. His fingers felt like clumsy sausages. The belt at his waist broke free and he leaned forward to work on the strap holding his legs.

The half-breed lifted Chavez off the ground, carried him several steps, and slammed him against the other cell. The female half-breed's arms drove through the bars and wrapped around Chavez's throat and she leaned back, strangling him. The male forced Chavez's left arm up and against the cell door, sliding it up and down as he had with his own cage until another chirp and clack echoed through the room.

"We have a breach," the doctor was yelling into the phone.

Mason kicked his legs out of the restraints and reached across his chest to free his left arm while he spun off the table and stood unevenly on the ground. The room wavered as much as he did, but he managed to focus on the task at hand and steady himself enough to concentrate on his last wrist restraint.

The female zombie burst out of her cell at a greyhound's pace, leaping and striding at full bore. The doctor hardly had time to hold her hands out to guard herself before the half-breed crashed into her. They slammed against the counter and tumbled over a line of chairs onto the ground.

Mason swallowed hard. The last restraint came off. The room still swam and he backed away from the table with the rigid, untested legs of a fawn taking his first steps. Mason watched the male half-breed let go of Chavez. He watched the sergeant slump to the ground against the bars. Mason took a step back, and then another as the male half-breed charged.

Mason glanced to his sides quickly, wondering where the pistol had fallen. He looked up again and saw only the eyes of hate hurtling at him.

Twenty

The pistol lay on the ground behind him. He had seen its black shell like a hole in the white tile flooring. The male half-breed took two last running steps before turning his shoulder into Mason's chest. He gasped at the impact, clamping his arms around the half-breed as they both careened out of control and into the wall of tempered glass. Mason tucked his chin just before his shoulders struck. The glass burst into a thousand unmoving shards behind him, leaving a dent where he hit. Mason slumped over the top of the half-breed, gasping for air. His weight alone was enough to topple them both to the floor.

Mason rolled off the half-breed in an effort to escape. It moved quickly, scrambling on hands and knees before leaping onto Mason's back. An arm wrapped around his neck before he had wits to stop it. The half-breed leaned back, choking Mason. Mason rose upright against the hold, grabbing the thing's arm with his hands and pulling it away. He took in a deep breath and leaned forward again. The pistol was just a few feet out of reach.

As if sensing Mason's intent, the half-breed reached its other hand over Mason's eyes and nose, raking and smashing. The pain against his nose caused Mason to turn his head, and as he did, the half-breed swung to the side and tried to roll. Mason felt the pendulum effect tip him. He didn't fight it. He pushed in the same direction, lifting himself off the ground in the process. As they turned, Mason's body twisted so that he was above the half-breed, and with all his weight, he fell backwards onto the beast.

This time, the half-breed gasped. Mason slammed his head back, cracking its nose. It loosened its grip on Mason's face and neck just long enough for Mason to roll sideways. He reached his arm out and felt the pistol. His fingers closed over it even as the half-breed dragged him back, pulling and hammering its fists on his arm.

Mason elbowed the half-breed in the chest while letting the pistol fall to the floor. It slid into his own chest and he curled his left arm to grab it, elbowing the half-breed with his right and guarding against its blows to his head. It reached after the gun, but Mason blocked it. The half-breed pummeled him mercilessly.

Mason worked the pistol into a proper hold. He aimed it haphazardly over his shoulder and pulled the trigger, not caring what he hit. *Blam!* He knew he missed, but he needed a second's respite. He was still so weak and clumsy and light headed. The half-breed flinched at the sudden noise. Mason rolled toward the half-breed and fired over his shoulder again. *Blam!* He wasn't sure if he hit the half-breed or not, but the thing pushed him away and Mason gladly rolled toward the glass wall, finally free of the thing's grip.

Mason spun and aimed at it, but didn't fire. It scurried away, diving behind the base of another operating table to avoid getting shot at. It must have thought the weapon only a Taser. If it had any idea that he could shoot it *through* the operating table, it would have kept fighting for its life.

Mason looked over at the opposite wall. The female half-breed had the doctor pinned and was leaning on the doctor's neck with her forearm as the doctor flailed at the half-breed's shoulders. Mason took aim and fired. *Blam!* The shot cracked a hole in the cabinet above their heads. The female half-breed looked across the room with a fiery gaze. Its eyes didn't register the danger. *Blam!* Mason fired another round which splintered the cabinet, breaking the wood in half and causing it to fall.

"Off," Mason warned, waving the pistol.

The half-breed growled but let up on the doctor. The doctor choked for air as the female half-breed leapt off her and bounded on hands and feet toward the other operating table to hide with the male. The doctor rolled on her side, coughing and taking in deep wheezing breaths. The two half-breeds cautiously peered around the wide bases of the operating table. They weren't mindless like normal zombies.

Mason used the wall to help him get to his feet. He staggered across the room, switching the pistol to his right hand to keep it aimed at the two hiding half-breeds. The doctor didn't try to get up. Her breathing was raspy and uneven. Mason reached down and grabbed her by her lab coat and shirt collar to drag her across the room. He pulled her nearly limp body to the far door and plucked her badge off her chest to swipe it over the locking mechanism. The door opened with a clack and Mason dragged her out into the hallway, letting the door shut behind them. He leaned against the glass on the opposite side of the hall, breathing hard, short of breath, light-headed, and feeling like he was going to throw up. His head swam and the world moved even though he didn't.

"Doc," Mason sighed. "Doc?" He looked at her badge. O'Farrell, W. It triggered nothing.

"Huh?" she replied, rolling onto her back, still gasping for air.

Mason dropped her card onto her chest. She put a hand over it.

"Doc, who did you call?" Mason managed

Plagued

to ask between breaths.

"Ken," she wheezed. "Kennedy."

He thumped the back of his head against the glass.

"Come on," he said. "You've got to get up. Come on."

"Where?" she managed to ask as she pushed herself to a sitting position.

"Nobody's coming," Mason told her. "Nobody'll come."

"What?"

"We've got to go."

"Where?"

"Anywhere but here."

Mason took a deep breath to fend off his nausea. He gulped down a lump in his throat before holding a hand out to the doctor. She reluctantly took it, and he hauled her to her unsteady feet. He put an arm around her waist to help steady her and they both looked in at the lab. Chavez lay on his back next to the cells, but otherwise the room looked empty.

"What about Chavez?"

"He's dead," Mason said.

"How do you know?"

"Because he deserves to be."

"We've got to go get him."

"He let them bite me," Mason said, glaring at her. "He did it on purpose."

"Chavez?" she asked, appearing horror struck as she looked up into Mason's eyes.

"Why?"

"I'm a liability," Mason said, pointing at his head. "They're gone, the things she said, but they're still in there. I feel it. They're there."

"Lieutenant," the doctor objected.

Mason held the pistol up and waved it toward the exit. "Just go," he said, grimacing at the pain in his head that came with trying to dredge up the memories of what he knew. They had sent him here. That much he remembered.

The doctor led them down the hall. Mason watched her and wondered what a pretty woman like her was doing in a place like this. She was a scientist, but why would anyone volunteer to be here? Maybe, like him, she wasn't a volunteer.

"I was sent here," Mason told her.

She looked over her shoulder with a questioning gaze.

"Someone gave me intelligence on everything. I know things I shouldn't. I met with Kennedy, I can't remember why or when, and she…I know it's in there. I know it's why they put me to work with Chavez. He killed his own men in Egypt. He shot them himself."

"Jones," the doctor said softly, trying to calm him with her soothing tone.

"Open the goddamned door," Mason said, pointing the pistol at her.

"Then what?"

"They told me not to trust her. I didn't listen," he said, shaking his head. "Open the door."

The doctor swiped her badge and the outer door blipped. Mason pushed her through it and they left the laboratory. Mason had her swipe her card at the stair access as well. As he walked under the rush of fans, he felt a jolt of recognition. The wind blew over him and he remembered his orientation with Chavez, how he called him names. No, that was someone else. Matty. Matty with the duck. The tattered pieces were maddening.

"Up," he said, pointing his pistol ahead of her, another wave of nausea striking him. He leaned forward and felt an upheaval.

"You're still sick, Jones," she told him. "You need to rest. We're safe here."

Mason vomited onto the wall, heaving repeatedly as the doctor held him around the waist so he wouldn't fall. Mason spat the taste from his mouth and wiped his lips with the back of his hand.

"Am I really cured?" Mason asked.

"That was what the blood test—"

"Am I a half-breed?" Mason snapped.

"No," she replied directly.

"Then why test me?"

"Your testosterone levels may inhibit some of your recovery. We've found in some cases that the subject regresses."

"So I'm not cured."

"No, you're cured. You won't become one of them, but…."

"But, what?"

"Several subjects died for no apparent reason," she told him softly, calmly. "That's why we haven't announced the cure. We're still trying to isolate the cause."

Mason said nothing. He struggled to remember the things he had known, to piece together what fragments of his past that could hold meaning to him now, to help him figure out why this was happening. It was infuriating to know he should know a thing but be unable to recall it. What did Kennedy tell him? He struck his head with his palm, closing his eyes, hoping to jar something.

"What's wrong?" the doctor asked. "Are you in pain?"

Mason opened his eyes to see her concern. She wasn't like the others. She wasn't part of their conspiracy—and it *was* a conspiracy, he knew it, although he couldn't remember why or how he knew. "I'm fine," he lied, waving the pistol toward the stairs leading up. "Move. We don't have much time."

Twenty-One

Mason staggered up the stairs, leaning against the railing and the wall, dragging his good shoulder along the smooth, cold concrete. The chill revived him and the solidity of the wall helped ground him so the spinning in his head didn't deceive him.

"How long will it take?" Mason asked the doctor.

"For what?"

"Until this fatigue wears off."

"Look, you need to lie down and rest. Your body has been through enormous trauma. The logistics of how long and—"

"Logistics!?" Mason echoed. A thread of memory appeared and he snatched it, yanking it in a frenzy of desperation, hauling the thought closer and closer...*this isn't the time to get into a discussion about logistics, Lieutenant*, Kennedy had said. *Entire states can be restored.* "Why didn't I see it?"

"See what?" the doctor asked.

"Can the cure be administered another way, like an airborne pathogen or gas or something? Something big like cloud seeding or…or…or with rats or deer or something."

"Probably. The original strain mutated from an airborne transmission pathway."

"What happens when you give the cure to normal people?"

"It doesn't give you an immunity, if that's what you're thinking."

"Does it kill normal people, too?" Mason asked as the doctor reached the landing.

"You're not going to die," she assured him, stopping to face him.

"Does the cure *harm* normal people?"

"We haven't encountered any cases," the doctor said. She backed up to lean against the door to the cell block.

Mason reached the top of the steps, still using the wall for support.

"You look terrible, Jones."

"Matches how I feel," he replied. He reached into his cargo pocket and pulled out his card. The door sensor beside him, the one that led to the interior offices, was blinking yellow. He swiped his card over it anyway. The sensor went red and chirped, then started blinking yellow again.

"Shit," he said, stuffing his card back into his pocket. He looked across at the door leading to the cell block. The sensor was solid red. "Open it," he said with a wave of the pistol. She looked at the door, then at Mason as though the idea were absurd.

Plagued

"Help is on its way," she argued.

"Really?" Mason asked skeptically. "How long ago did you call Kennedy? Five minutes?"

"It takes time to get into the facility."

"There are guards already *in* the facility, on the roof, on the outer wall, at the gate tower. Where are they? Where did Johnson go? Why isn't the alarm going off?"

"Let's calm down," she said. "You've had significant brain trauma because of the consumption pathogen. Things that seem perfectly reasonable to you right now are *not* necessarily reality."

"I can still tell time," Mason said sharply. "Why hasn't anyone come?"

"They're—" she said, but couldn't finish her answer.

"That's the last door she can lock out remotely. Let's get through it."

The doctor didn't move.

"Doctor, please," Mason said.

She sighed and swiped her card over the reader. Mason held his breath. The light blinked red and it chirped. There was a loud clack and Mason sighed as the air fans started and the door began to roll open.

"Come on," Mason ordered, taking her arm as he passed through the door. The moaning in the cell block erupted as it always did, and at the far end he saw the bloody remnants of the accident. No, it was no accident, he told himself. Chavez freed that biter. Even if it was just an accident because he was lazy, then he was still guilty. It was that same laziness that got his squad killed in Egypt.

Mason reached the first cell door and let the doctor go. She shook her arm free and stepped away from him, away from the cells and toward the safety of the center of the room.

"Run on down there to the rolling gates," Mason told her. He saw the yellow blinking lights on the door sensors from here. The building was in lockdown. Even though Kennedy hadn't sent for help, she *had* sealed the facility. Mason knew *someone* was coming, and they wouldn't be *any* help. "Hit the red alarm button next to the door."

"What? Why?"

"Because," Mason said, digging his hand into his cargo pocket to withdraw his access card again. "This is an emergency." He swiped his card over the cell door sensor. It beeped and buzzed, and the door jerked open under the weight of the zombie that was leaning against it.

Mason walked straight toward the next cell door, looking up at one of the video cameras mounted on the ceiling. If he was going to break through the lockdown, he needed zombies. An army of them.

"Wait," the doctor said desperately, taking

several frightened steps toward the rolling gate door. Two zombies stepped out of the cell, lurching toward her in a slow shamble.

Mason swiped his card on the next door and kept walking.

"Run," he shouted at her. His command startled some sense into her and she bolted into a run. Mason slid his card on the next cell, then the next, freeing cell after cell of biters. They shambled out in a wave of slow moving death following in his wake. He didn't tell her that he was freeing only the safe zombies, the ones that already had their glands removed. The only danger with this bunch was their appetite. The other hundred or more biters on the other side of the cell block were best left behind bars.

The doctor reached the door and whacked the button. The alarm began to wail and all the biters ducked in a collective fright. Mason continued to open cells as he marched toward her. She was frantically waving her card over the door sensor, trying to escape.

"It won't open," she shouted, turning and pressing her back to the wall. She tried both the rolling gate sensor and the man-door sensor, and neither worked. She looked back at Mason, riveted to the spot with fear.

"Don't worry," Mason called, swiping his card over the last cell he planned on opening. He had opened over a dozen, and behind him there were at least thirty biters roaming freely.

That would be enough. He couldn't run. Walking was taxing enough. The room tilted and he found himself trying to correct for it, leaning as he marched, his sight set on the yellow button next to the red one. Hands reached out toward him and he edged toward the center of the room to avoid leaning in their direction.

"The door won't open," the doctor screamed when Mason finally reached her.

"Close your eyes," Mason yelled back at her as he reached a hand out and pressed the yellow button. It triggered the bug zappers, or so Matty called them. High luminosity LEDs mounted throughout the cell block erupted like a thousand flashbulbs, pulsing with rhythmic strobe, forcing Mason to close his eyes as he put his hands on the wall to steady himself. The flashing light had the same effect on the zombies. Their moans became groans of anguish, and although Mason couldn't see them, he knew they were all raising arms to cover their heads, maybe even swinging blindly at their formless assailant.

"Jesus," the doctor swore.

"It only lasts ten seconds," Mason said loud enough to be heard over the wailing of the hundreds of tortured zombies. The white flashes suddenly ceased and the patchwork of spots in the darkness of his closed eyes began to swim and glide in his vision. He opened his eyes and still felt partially blinded. The wailing of the alarm kept blaring, echoing in the cell block, drowning out in rhythmic fashion the dazed groans of the zombies. Mason turned around to see most of the ones he had freed collapsed on the ground. Several were flailing their arms randomly.

"It stuns them for about a minute or two," Mason told her. He reached past her and took a fire extinguisher off the wall, pushing it into her hands. "When they get close, use this to confuse them."

"What!?"

"Standard protocol is for the wall guard to be first responders. They have the clearance to override a lockdown."

"But a lockdown only occurs when an alarm is raised," she argued. "We could have just gone out if you hadn't made me press that button!"

"Kennedy already had us in a lockdown. Why do you think I couldn't get through that other door?"

"Your card's been deactivated," she reasoned "They knew you've been bit!"

"Really? Then how come I can open the cell doors?"

Her mouth was open, but she didn't answer.

"They'll be here within five minutes," Mason assured her. "But this might be close."

Twenty-Two

Strange how his memories tumbled and rolled like the liquid in a wave machine. He remembered some of his conversation with Kennedy, and he had an idea now of why he had been sent here. Someone had wanted him to come shut it down, but how anyone would go about shutting down a facility like Biter's Island was unfathomable.

The path of that thought careened into a wall. How was he even supposed to get out of this place in one piece? He stared at the zombies he had let escape from their cells, blinking to recover his full sight, still dazed by his ordeal. The zombies began to sit up or roll to their knees one by one. They looked lost, like the soldiers in the mess hall of the psych ward he'd been sent to after the Egypt incident. The military hospital he had been stationed at. He sat alone, staring at a television that played some breaking news. It showed images of columns of smoke that rose on the other side of a wide river behind a newsman who told of a tragedy at a Breckenrock Corporation facility inside the Plagued States. A helicopter roared over the newsman, making the newsman duck with a hand over his head as though the chopper might actually hit him. The camera panned to watch it race across the channel.

"That was close, Phil. Are you OK?"

"Yes, we're fine here," the newsman replied while waving a hand toward the chopper. "But as you can see, rescue crews like that one have been making regular runs across the channel for hours looking for survivors. And we're told that there *have* been survivors, but the concern right now is that contaminated individuals may have been thrown into the channel by the earlier explosions, so authorities have been warning all towns and cities along the channel to alert them of any survivors, or their bodies, that wash up on shore and to avoid contact with them at all cost.

"Also, the Army is still enforcing the no-fly zone and there are at least a dozen shore patrol boats in the water looking for survivors, as well as keeping all watercraft out of the area.

"I don't know if you can see it, but there are literally twenty or more drones flying down the shoreline, specifically looking for victims of the explosion who may have been thrown into the channel…."

Mason scooped his lunch, spooning it slowly and purposefully into his mouth as he stared over the heads of his fellow soldiers in the mess hall, all equally glued to the scene.

The footage didn't strike him as real, as though it was just another replaying of old footage. For Mason, the television reports first started in grade school, but by the time he finished high school he was studying the origins and immediate effects of the outbreak. Endless reports and papers on the same thing, over and over again. A monotonous drilling, like scooping the bland potatoes into his mouth.

"Thank you for that report, Phil," the anchorwoman said as the picture changed to a video showing an aerial approach of the affected area. "What we're seeing now is exclusive drone video footage obtained from the Skywatch blog," she continued.

Mason stopped chewing, staring with sudden interest at the video feed. He recognized the appearance of the hundreds of scorching blasts enveloping the hillside. The sheer volume of craters scoring the ground made it appear like the surface of the moon, but with blasts so close together it looked more like a carpet bombing, levelling the entire hillside and every building, shattering even concrete foundations, toppling the ring wall that once held back the rest of the Plague States.

The sentry ring.

Mason's thoughts returned to the present. He wondered if that's what they wanted him to do. Blow this place sky high? It would make sense. How else do you put an end to the slave trade except to destroy the places where the trade is sanctioned?

Mason couldn't believe that they thought he would help them blow up this facility up. Blowing the sentry ring would kill everyone, his fellow soldiers included.

"Are you married?" Mason asked the doctor. O'Farrell's name sounded Irish, and with her red hair he suspected it was her own name.

"What?" Her incredulous expression turned in his direction.

"I'll get you home to your family, is all I mean. I owe you my life."

"No, I'm not married," she said tersely, shaking her head. Her eyes softened. She adjusted the fire extinguisher in her hands. "You?"

"No," Mason said with a sigh. "At least, I don't think so."

A brief laugh escaped with a grin. Her smile faded as quickly as her breath. Several of the zombies were on their feet again and slowly lurching toward them, still dazed, but with enough sense to hone in on their voices.

"Spray the face," Mason instructed, pointing at the fire extinguisher. "They hate it. Wait until they're less than ten feet away. Don't waste that stuff."

"Can't we hit that light show again?"

"Not until the zappers recharge."

"How long does that take?"

"About five minutes," Mason told her. They both shook their heads.

Across the cell block someone appeared in the open doorway of the stairwell. It was Johnson. He froze in his tracks at the sight of the freed zombies. Mason tapped the doctor and pointed him out. Johnson's mouth uttered curses as he backed out of sight.

"So much for *his* help."

Mason levelled his pistol at an approaching biter and took aim. *Blam!* A collective flinching rolled through the cell block like a wave. The noise echoed long after the biter fell to its side, collapsing over its shot out leg.

"Why didn't you kill it?!"

"We're not allowed to use lethal force," Mason replied.

"What idiot thought that up?"

Mason turned to face her, wondering why her words felt so familiar in his own mind, as though he had recently thought it himself. He looked back at the flailing biter, at the blood smearing across the tile. He saw more biters behind it. He struggled to recall why this scene seemed so familiar. He knew how he had been bit. The remnants of *that* struggle were still plain to see. Mason lifted his pistol again and took aim on another biter. The shock of recognition jolted him physically and he lowered his aim.

Matty killed himself. He'd been bitten, so he killed himself. He didn't know about the cure. Only that man—the hunter named Opland—only he knew. He had a beer and a duck and a half-breed. Was it his half-breed downstairs?

Mason hit his forehead with the palms of his hands, the pistol butt striking the crown of his eye. Why couldn't he remember things the way they happened, or even at all?

"Jones," the doctor said anxiously. "Don't freak out on me now. They're getting closer!"

Mason wrung out his eyes. Nothing came. No memories, no tears, no rage. He opened them and took aim on the first biter. *Blam!* The bullet knocked its head back and splattered blood in the air behind it. O'Farrell was right about killing them. It was a stupid rule. The zombie fell backwards, collapsing over its legs to its side. Mason took aim on another. *Blam!* It fell with a life-ending bullet through the skull, a spray of gore and blood erupting behind it, painting the ground and two other biters.

Like sharks worked into a frenzy, several biters fell over the dead.

"This won't make a lot of sense, but I have to tell somebody. It's driving me crazy," Mason said. The doctor looked at him with caution. "Kennedy enlisted me to help close this place. I remember that much. Someone else assigned me here, *for her*. God, I wish I could remember who. They gave me information about how to blow this place up."

"Jones," the doctor said, her voice wavering as she tried to control her fear.

"I have to tell you," Mason cut her off.

"You may be confusing some of your memories," the doctor said over him.

"Doc," Mason growled. He looked at the biters that were moving past the two he had killed and took aim on one. *Blam!* The biter collapsed where it stood and two more advancing biters fell over it, greedy for the taste of flesh. Beyond the wall of carnage, twenty other biters shuffled to move around the blockade.

Mason levelled his glare on the doctor. "We don't have a lot of time. I don't know what's going to happen to me once they get here, but Kennedy wants me dead, or at least out of the way. Let me ask you, what do they do with people like me? People who have been cured?"

"Rehabilitation," the doctor replied. "There's a clinic on the Rurals side where we keep several under observation."

The word knocked him so hard it jarred another thread of memory to the surface.

"You're only here for observation," Doctor Liu had said months ago, maybe years by now.

Liu wore an Army uniform, rank of colonel. He tried to seem friendly, but wore the fatigued look of a man with too many responsibilities to be genuinely interested in one man's problems. Was it even really a problem at all, Mason had wondered.

"How long do I have to be here?" Mason had asked him.

"Until you're fit for duty again," Colonel Liu replied with a disarming smile.

Until you think I'm ready, you mean, Mason remembered thinking. Who gets to decide what "fit" meant anyway?

"Did I do something wrong?" Mason asked.

"Why don't you tell me what you think? Do you think you did something wrong?"

"I killed a fellow soldier, sir."

"That's right, but you didn't exactly answer the question, now, did you, lieutenant?"

"Well, neither did you, doc."

The doctor smiled and looked down to write in his notes.

Mason remembered now. He had killed a man in Egypt. It wasn't Chavez who had killed his men. Mason had killed one of his own. The crazy thing was, he couldn't remember ever having done it in the first place, but the feeling was there, as though guilt had been feeding on him, ripping apart his mind and spirit. Just like the consumption pathogen was crippling him.

"You know why I'm back home, right?" Mason heard himself asking, the memory of his voice echoing just above the drone of the hundreds of zombies in the cell block.

"Yeah, I do. That's kind of the point," the driver that had ferried him from and to the airport said.

"They don't care about me," Mason gasped in realization.

"What?" Doctor O'Farrell asked. "Jones, snap out of it!"

"They never cared about my photographic memory."

"Jones," the doctor pleaded, staring up at him, putting a hand on his shoulders.

"They only cared about my record," Jones told her. "They let me get bit so they could pin destroying the place on me. An unstable, disgruntled soldier."

"Jones, the gates," O'Farrell yelled, shaking him by the shoulder. She let his arm go and pointed. The haze of thought blurred and Mason looked into her frantic eyes. She turned her attention toward the cell block, flush with despair.

"The doors all buzzed open!"

She was right. The cell doors were all opening. Biters on both sides of the aisle were stumbling out of confinement.

Twenty-Three

Holding your ground on a wall amidst a line of twenty soldiers as hundreds of angry civilian protesters poured into the square was one thing. Standing alone against over two hundred blood-thirsty zombies with only a pistol and a prayer was another. Mason stepped in front of the doctor to shield her anyway. He was her only chance.

"They're all open," O'Farrell said hysterically. "How did they do that? Why?"

Mason didn't answer. He looked over his shoulder to see her low hanging shoulders, the defeat even in her posture.

"Three minutes," Mason told her.

"Three!? We won't last one!"

Mason looked back at the horde and aimed toward one of the infectious behind the leaders, a big body that lurched slowly, it eyes lost in a white haze. *Blam!* The zombie's head snapped back as a spray of gore burst over the eager biters behind it. They followed the body down. Several biters in front turned, slowing to decide whether the carcass was worth fighting over. The whole horde slowed with them, unable to lurch free of their collective gridlock.

Mason held his aim, selecting his next target. Not until they all start moving again, he thought. Several of the lead biters turned to try to get to Mason's last victim. Like dogs, they growled at one another, pushing and shoving each other over inches of space. The largest of the lead zombies bullied his way into the circle, wrenching another off the body. Two other zombies stumbled over the newly fallen and again the wall came to a halt.

"Shoot another one," O'Farrell suggested.

"Not yet," Mason said over his shoulder. "This pistol only holds fifteen rounds."

Mason stepped closer to the door and banged on the yellow button again, the one that triggered the bug zappers. He hoped they had recharged by now. Nothing happened.

Several of the lead zombies broke free of their pack and fanned out wide around the bodies covering the floor. The flow of biters had resumed. Mason stepped in front of O'Farrell again and raised his pistol once more, sighting what he thought might be his next target.

The door chirped, and both Mason and the doctor looked toward it. It burst open and two soldiers rushed in, each leading with Tasers. As they swept, the weapons turned in both directions. One fired. *Snap!* Mason's eyes bulged. The pins rushed through the air, streaming out a thin line of silk. Both needles struck the doctor in the chest and she began to convulse.

"We're human," Mason shouted, holding his hands in the air. "We're human. Shit."

The fire extinguisher fell out of the doctor's hands and clanked onto the concrete as she toppled. Two more soldiers pushed through the door, each carrying noose poles. Mason caught the doctor as she slumped over, worried he would be struck with a residual shock.

"Hold the door," one of the soldiers, a sergeant, shouted behind him. His head swiveled to survey the scene.

The soldier who had shot the doctor ejected the strings from his weapon and turned it toward the biters without a word. Mason held her by the armpits and turned her, dragging her toward the door.

"Get her out," the sergeant ordered Mason. "Set the line. Taze any that close in."

Mason yanked the pins and wires from the doctor's chest and dragged her through the door. The last remaining soldier pushed past him and the door closed behind him, leaving Mason alone with the unconscious doctor in the dark courtyard.

Mason took a deep breath, his eyes wide from the adrenaline coursing through his veins. It kept him standing, at least. He knew it wouldn't last, though. He lifted the doctor into his arms and looked around.

Mason stumbled across the courtyard with Doctor O'Farrell draped in his arms, toward what looked like Chavez's Jeep. He trudged as fast as he could, listing one way for a dozen steps, then listing the other, his dizziness playing with his perception. To counteract the effect, he focused on one thought: reach the Jeep without dropping her. The alarm wailed from horns mounted on the roof of the prison complex. It was so loud he doubted anyone on the island would still be asleep.

Mason's arms gave out as he lifted O'Farrell's limp body into the Jeep. He collapsed onto her as she fell into the seat. He stood with his weight propping her up, breathing hard, trying not to vomit all over her. He felt a wave of nausea lifting to his throat, but he swallowed it down and let out his breath. It worked to calm his stomach, but his head began to spin wildly. His eyes tumbled like a Newton's cradle, swinging downward toward the center of his vision, only to be whacked back up to the right by his other eyeball.

He defied the illusion of his senses and straightened, pushing the doctor against the seat. He grabbed the latch on the seat and leaned her back so she wouldn't slump forward. Buckling her in brought another wave of nausea he again fought off. He used his hands to guide him around the hood of the vehicle.

The keys were on the seat. The engine turned over easily and Mason backed them away from the wall, then turned the wheel and raced them toward the gate. The vehicle lights came on automatically. He took a wide turn to drive up beside a call box in front of the gate through the outer wall, the one called the Inside Passage.

Mason honked on the horn several times. He looked over at the doctor, still out cold and unaffected by the noise.

"Report," a voice said through the call box.

"We shot this woman with a Taser," Mason said, not looking toward the device. He suspected it had a camera. "She's one of the lab workers. I've got to get her to the infirmary."

The call box went silent and Mason wondered what kind of lie he might be able to concoct if pressed, or if he should tell them his own identity and give them his card. The one thing he did know was that any minute the door would open regardless and the rest of the response team would come pouring through.

The gate opened, empty to his surprise. He drove into the man-trap and stopped to wait for the gate to close behind him.

"Turn off your lights," a voice said through a speaker and Mason killed the engine. The gate boomed shut behind him and the blacklights above hummed. Up until this very moment, it hadn't occurred to Mason that he might register as a zombie, or that his eyes might be glowing as though someone had stuffed two little flashlights behind them. He leaned forward to look in the rear view mirror, but saw nothing but the bloody abrasions just below his eyes. He sighed with relief and heard the buzzing of the other door ahead of him.

He turned over the engine and put it in gear as light from other vehicles beyond the gate cast over him. Men came through on foot alongside the wall, each outfitted with full body armor, helmets, Tasers, hand-guns, and catching noose poles. Mason pushed past the gate and drove onto the sidewalk to get out of the way of the queue trying to get in.

He took another deep breath and felt a wave of relief wash over him. The beams of his Jeep shone across the main road onto one of the Quonset huts, and his relief waned. What if this got out of hand? Someone had let out all the zombies. There were thirty men going back in there to try to contain nearly two hundred zombies.

Mason turned in his seat to look into the man-trap tunnel. The third Jeep edged in just ahead of the door closing behind it. Mason spun around again to look out over the base. He knew the head count on Rock Island. Even though it was a twenty-four hour facility, only ninety-six soldiers were stationed on base at any given time. Mason gauged that number against The Rule. Two-to-one odds against all those zombies, which was more than sufficient to consider it overwhelming force, but at least they were contained to the prison complex.

The street ahead looked deserted except for the lights of another approaching vehicle. Mason waited for it to pass, leaning over the doctor.

"Doc." Mason gently slapped her face. She didn't stir.

The other vehicle came out from behind the line of buildings, another open-top Jeep. Mason sat upright again to put his own vehicle into gear. His headlights lit up the passing Jeep and Mason clearly made out the warden and Kennedy in the front seats. Another Jeep followed, then another. The driver of the third looked familiar too, but Mason couldn't place him. His memories were too muddled.

The three Jeeps raced toward the bridge leading to the Rurals, toward civilization. Like the prison complex, the bridge leading to the Rurals had a bus-length vehicular man-trap. Enough for three Jeeps, but not four.

"Shit," Mason hissed. "They're bugging out. Doc, wake up!"

The three Jeeps came to a stop in front of the bridge gate. Mason considered his options.

He could force his way. There was room in the other vehicles. The thought only lasted a second, though. The Quonset huts ahead of him, the ones he knew held the sentry ring, yawned open to the night sky with a metallic creak.

"They're going to blow the place," Mason groaned. He grabbed the doctor's lab coat and shirt at the shoulder as he lurched the vehicle forward. He winced in pain as he turned the wheel using only his left arm. "Doc, come on, wake up!"

Mason rounded the corner, accelerating toward the Meat Market. Several street lights shone over the nearly empty sidewalks. Two soldiers jogged across the road to avoid being hit. The checkpoint gate went across the road. It was just a wooden guard post. The soldier inside the checkpoint building leaned out, but retreated as Mason revved the engine to burst through the post. It cracked across the hood and windshield.

Mason felt the doctor stiffen. He looked over at her. His hand was still holding her shoulder so she wouldn't slip. Her head turned side to side in the near darkness.

"What was that? Where am I?"

"Doc," Mason said with relief. "Kennedy is bugging out. We've got to get the hell off the island."

"Jones?" she asked, turning her head

toward him. She put her hand on his where he still gripped her coat and shirt. He felt her lean forward as she tried to sit upright. "Ow! My chest."

"We're almost there," Mason told her, not letting go of her shirt. He let off the gas and coasted past the Meat Market, then slowed to take a wide turn into the parking lot behind it.

"What are we doing here?"

Mason clicked on his high beams as he drove between the two lines of parked slaver rigs. Only two rows could fit in the lot because of their length and size. Mason knew the one that would stand out was the duck, the vehicle he was looking for. He hoped it would still be here.

"Jones, slow down," O'Farrell said anxiously.

Mason plied the brakes and the Jeep ground to a halt over the loose dirt lot. Mason took a deep breath, relieved at seeing the duck's narrow nose sticking out of the long line of squared engines. Mason blew the Jeep's horn.

"Jones," the doctor said as he stepped out of the Jeep, blowing the horn again. She looked around nervously.

Mason started around the front of the vehicle. He felt another wave of nausea and dizziness wash over him.

"Hank, are you up there?" Mason called

weakly. He leaned against the hood of the Jeep for support, looking up at the bow of the duck.

O'Farrell rushed to Mason's side, putting her arms around his waist and sliding her head under his arm to help him stand.

"Hank!"

"Who is it?" the old slaver asked, leaning over the rail above with a blanket around his shoulders. "Kid, you look like shit!"

"Jones," the doctor whispered. "What are we doing?"

"Hank," Mason called to the slaver. "We need help. We need out." Mason started walking the length of the duck with O'Farrell's help.

"Hang on, kid," Hank said, shrugging off his blanket to follow them toward the back of the vehicle. Mason's strength gave out. He knelt down and tried to concentrate on breathing. The doctor removed herself from under his arm and knelt beside Mason. He dry heaved again, falling forward onto his hands. His whole body felt weak to the point that any moment he might collapse without the strength to even breathe.

"Kid, what's wrong?" Hank asked anxiously.

"Jones, you need rest," O'Farrell said.

"And who's she?" Hank asked gruffly. "Who are you?" He glared down at O'Farrell.

"She's with me," Mason said between

quick breaths. His arms went limp and he fell onto his right side, gasping. Hank hovered high over them both, watching warily. "We need to get off the island."

"Kid," Hank prodded.

"Right now," Mason called as he rolled to his knees, fighting to recapture his lost strength. O'Farrell leaned down to help him. "No time to explain."

Across the island there came a bright light followed by a deep, rumbling boom.

"What was that?" Hank asked, standing straight to look toward the sound. It came from the prison complex.

"Start the engine," Mason called as he used O'Farrell to help lift himself to his feet. Even she neglected him a moment to stare with surprise toward the light.

"Yeah," Hank replied distantly. "Yeah, good idea."

Mason and O'Farrell moved quickly to the back ladder. Against his dizziness, Mason managed to hook his feet and arms from rung to rung as the glow plugs of the diesel engine buzzed beneath the big vehicle.

"Start the engine," Mason shouted as he flopped over the rail and onto the deck. Hank was at the driver's seat flipping switches. O'Farrell shimmied up the ladder and crouched beside Mason.

"Come on," she whispered, tugging on

him. He nodded and allowed her to guide him forward as the starter chugged and whined, but the engine refused to come to life. It clacked and wheezed as Hank let off on the key. Mason fell into the passenger seat, leaving O'Farrell standing between them as another bright flash lit the sky, followed by a rumbling boom.

Hank turned the key again. The starting motor whinnied and whirred as the engine chugged and skipped, grumbling out of tune, refusing to start. Hank let off on the key again.

"You've got to be kidding me," the doctor said.

Twenty-Four

The duck wouldn't start.

"Shit," Hank growled, hitting the steering wheel.

O'Farrell sank to her knees. She looked at Mason with regret. "I thought you were just being paranoid," she said softly. "About blowing the place up."

"Shit, shit, shit," Hank hissed in cadence with the sputtering engine as the starter turned over and over. "Come on, you piece of junk!"

Another round of bright flashes lit the hemline of horizon on the other side of the island. The echoing boom of several more explosions followed.

"What was that?" the doctor asked, her eyes turning toward the glow.

"The bridge," Mason guessed.

The duck growled and chugged to life. A thick fog of black smoke washed over them past the front of the duck, heavy with the fumes of burnt fuel, dissolving as it passed through the still lit headlights of the Jeep. Hank ground the duck into gear and it lurched forward, grazing the front of the Jeep. The doctor fell sideways, losing her balance. Mason grabbed her and pulled her into his lap. The light of the Jeep reflecting up the side of the duck lit her eyes and Mason could plainly see her shock.

Hank cranked the wheel, and the duck turned abruptly. O'Farrell threw an arm around Mason's neck for support. The nose of the duck barely missed the rigs parked in front of them as the whole vehicle swung to the right.

"Where are you going?" the doctor asked frantically.

"Toward the beach," Mason answered for Hank. "We need to get into the water."

"What beach?" O'Farrell looked out the windshield ahead of them as Hank turned on the floodlights. The parking lot woke under their beams. A row of orange and red reflectors from the two dozen or so rigs lit their path like a runway, and Hank accelerated with his foot on the floor.

Mason flinched at the *thump, tizzzz* sound, turning to see a trail of fiery red catapulting skyward. Another *thump, tizzzz* went off, then another, and another. All four trails raced toward the stars.

"What is that?" O'Farrell asked in astonishment, her head craned back so she could look straight up. Hank didn't take his eyes off the road ahead. The duck turned again at the end of the lot and bounced up a curb, missing a small tree that scratched and hissed down the side of the vehicle as they raced by.

"Cluster bombs," Mason told her.

"Why are they going up?"

"You don't want to know," Mason replied grimly. Another *thump, tizzzz* went off. "Hank, step on it!"

"It's floored!"

The duck fell into and bounded out of a shallow gully meant for water runoff. Mason recognized the wide expanse of grass that they landed on. Another *thump, tizzzz* lit up the sky.

"That way," Mason said, pointing toward a building he vaguely remembered.

"I know, I know," Hank cried.

Another *thump, tizzzz* went off, and once more. Mason clenched his teeth and looked up to see the sky littered with red contrails.

The green of the grass in the wash of their floodlights gave way to blackness.

"There," Mason shouted, pointing. O'Farrell turned her attention forward. Mason looked up. A false sun lit the sky, a strobe, like streaks of lightning. It sparkled as one after another the cluster bombs began to erupt. Now instead of only a few missiles falling back toward the island, Mason knew there were likely a hundred smaller, more deadly warheads fanning out to destroy every square inch of land.

Mason gripped O'Farrell's waist tighter.

"Hold on," Hank warned. He didn't slow

down. Mason reached over his shoulder for the seat belt only to find there wasn't one. He braced his legs against the floorboard and put one arm onto the dashboard. O'Farrell leaned forward and put her hands on the dash, turning her head to look at Mason with a desperate plea of forgiveness.

Mason only nodded. He couldn't tell her they would survive. He doubted it himself. Her eyes were grim in the glow of the spotlights mounted above the windshield. She nodded as well and turned her gaze ahead.

The duck's nose pitched off the edge of the grass and onto the gravel beach. Behind him, he heard the *boom* of the first bombs hitting their targets. Stones rattled beneath the wheels of the duck and the vehicle bounced its nose upward again. It felt like the vehicle knew the danger and was trying to leap out onto the water as far as it could fling itself. Mason felt himself coming off his seat as they cruised through the air.

More rockets landed behind them, a rattling and insistent knocking and *booming* sound that shook the very air. The duck slammed to a halt. O'Farrell slumped forward in his grip. His legs burned at the effort of keeping himself from careening forward. His arm gave for a second, but he managed to hold on without crushing O'Farrell against the dashboard.

Plagued

The vehicle lurched the other way, and Mason felt himself snapped back into the seat. He hauled the doctor with him. Her elbows dug into his shoulders as she tried to slow herself.

The duck's bow carved a line of water into the air that fell over the vehicle as it plunged into the channel, drenching them from head to toe.

More explosions snapped and boomed all around. Fiery heat poured over them in waves, so strong the air itself grew heavier, driving them further into their seats.

Hank pushed himself off the steering wheel. He coughed as he worked two levers with his left hand and rubbed his chest with the right.

"You OK?" Mason asked. More explosions erupted behind them, setting off a chain reaction so loud they each covered their ears. Heat seared over them from a fireball that rolled and toppled out over the channel, rising as it churned and rumbled. More explosions began to strike further inland, blanketing the southern edge in a wave of fire.

Explosions hit so close, Mason hardly registered the noise from the ringing in his ears. A tree along the shoreline burst into burning fragments that flailed the duck in clanks and clatter, swatting them with twigs and branches and stones that cracked into the slave pens behind them.

The duck growled as the engine revved. Hank turned the wheel to straighten their course, moving them away from the burning shoreline as quickly as the lumbering vehicle could manage. The current did the rest of the work, ferrying them west along the length of the island. Bombs continued to strike quickly. Some landed in the channel, blowing water and fire into the air.

One burst off their port side, and the doctor screamed in Mason's arms as water sprayed over them, dousing the scorching heat from the fires at their backs.

"Can't this thing go any faster?" the doctor screamed. Even her voice was drowned out by the crack and boom of missile after missile blanketing the island.

Hank didn't answer. He couldn't hear her. His gnashed-tooth grimace and white knuckle grip of the steering wheel said everything, though.

Mason didn't watch the carpet bombing. He looked ahead and downstream at the broken bridge.

"Hank," Mason warned, pointing forward. "The bridge!"

Hank hazarded a brief glance, then a double-take. The 2nd Street Bridge had been blown, but the collapsed part stuck out of the channel at an angle as though it had only partially collapsed, leaving just a narrow opening to navigate through.

"God hates us," Hank reasoned aloud as he turned the wheel to steer the duck directly at the bridge.

Twenty-Five

The firestorm had passed, its rumble still shaking the earth. The surface of the surrounding channel vibrated. Mason wiped the sweat from his brow with the back of his hand. Hank switched the duck to reverse throttle and revved the engine in an effort to slow them down.

O'Farrell eased herself from Mason's lap, settling down on her knees between the two chairs. The fireball rising above them hissed and roared, its orange glow dimly lighting the world around them. The obstruction at the bridge was easy to see under the glow. Hank used the extra light to drive the duck against the current as he tried to aim them for the only span that looked wide enough for them to pass.

"Will we even fit?" O'Farrell asked as she looked through the front window at the approaching blockade.

Mason stood to look over the windshield at the top of the bridge. He thought he had seen movement. A *whit-dit-dit-dit* noise echoed over the *ting-tang-ring* of bullets swatting through the metal cages on the deck of the duck.

Mason pushed O'Farrell down by the back of her head. He collapsed over her while pushing her toward the foot well of the cockpit. Hank slid out of his seat and onto the floorboard in one motion.

"They're shooting at us!" O'Farrell uttered in disbelief.

"At least it's not helicopters," Hank grumbled. "I can't see where we're going. We're sitting ducks."

Mason crawled out and sat down behind the driver's seat, turning to face the oncoming bridge. He drew his pistol and held it to his knee as he leaned back against the cage.

"Guide us a little more left," Mason said. Hank turned the wheel from under the dash. "Give it some gas," Mason added as he lifted his head a little to see out over the seat back.

Ting-ting-tang came another spray of bullets just over Mason's head as the machine gunner on the bridge let out another *whit-dit-dit* burst. Mason ducked and shifted his position, adjusting his aim, anticipating where his target would appear when the bridge platform reached its apex above them.

"Are we going to crash?" Hank asked worriedly.

"Just five more seconds," Mason replied, blinking hard to drive the sweat from his eyes.

"What's happening?"

"Five more seconds," Mason insisted.

Tang-cling-clang-ping came another spray of bullets over the cages. Mason saw the flash of the other shooter's gun crest the dashboard. *Pong-ting-ting* came another burst. Mason leaned into the shot. *Blam!* His pistol kicked in his hand and he watched his target retreat.

"Shit," Mason hissed.

"What!?" Hank asked, starting to climb out.

"I missed," Mason said hotly.

Hank eased back under the dashboard.

The form appeared again, this time hovering over a slab of concrete giving him partial cover. The machine gun poured another volley of bullets over them, hammering the deck. *Thump-pap-crack-ting-snap* came the bullets as they gnawed their way toward Mason's prone position.

Mason took aim and a deep breath. *Blam!*

The machine gun abruptly stopped firing and Mason let out his breath.

"Did you get him?" Hank asked wildly.

The duck suddenly lurched, scraping against the pier along its port side before slamming to a halt. It was a jarring impact that knocked both the doctor and Hank back beneath the dash. Mason careened from his position, rolling and slamming into the driver seatback.

Hank clambered out from beneath the

dashboard, lifting himself into the seat with the aid of the steering wheel. The duck was aground on the partially collapsed bridge. The vehicle groaned and scraped as the strong current of the channel pushed them higher up the embankment. Hank laid into the throttle. The duck's engine growled as the whole vehicle shook, even though they hardly moved.

"We need to get off this mess," Hank growled as loudly as the engine.

O'Farrell crawled out to Mason, who still lay on his back, his legs open in a "V", his pistol pointing toward the intact portion of bridge on the Rurals side.

"Are you OK?" O'Farrell asked as she put a hand on his chest, tapping at him as she worked her hands over his body in the quest for blood.

"He's not alone," Mason told her and she froze, her head craning to look up at the bridge. Light shined out over the channel from some vehicle far out of sight. Two black shadows carved the light in half for a moment as they crossed the beams.

The duck turned sideways, dipping its port side against the pier as the starboard side lifted to clear the obstruction of the partially toppled bridge. The side of the duck raked the concrete pier as the vehicle's wheels found traction. The duck surged forward, shaking O'Farrell off her hands and knees. Mason slammed his elbow into the cage beside him to keep from sliding to the port rail. O'Farrell fell onto Mason and he grabbed her with his left hand to keep her from sliding away, too.

"If we get out of this alive," O'Farrell lamented in his ear, but let the sentiment trail off.

The grating noise of the duck scraping along the pier grew louder as the engine roared. The nose of the duck dipped awkwardly as a crack and pop noise burst from beneath the deck. The scraping died out and Mason felt the deck fall from beneath his shoulders. For a second, his stomach turned. He thumped onto the deck again as it lurched side to side.

"We're free!" Hank yelled.

A *whit-dit-dit-dit* answered his euphoria. Bullets sprayed over the roof of the rig, pinging off and snapping through the overhead lights and supply rack. *Blam!* Mason answered, not aiming at anything in particular. A warning shot to whoever was above, something to ease the attack long enough for Mason to find them.

Mason pushed O'Farrell off as he sat up, the pistol leading the way. The bridge receded above from the swift current below and the throbbing growl of the duck's diesel. Hank slid beneath the dashboard again, letting the vehicle find its own course, his hand wedging the gas pedal to the floor.

Another *whit-dit-dit* was quickly answered

by a *Blam!* A man screamed in pain, yelling "I'm hit, I'm hit," repeatedly. More bullets sprayed over them from two machine guns on the bridge. The rounds whacked against the cages filling the back half of the duck. *Tings, tangs,* and *cracks* splattered the vehicle like hailstones.

Blam!

"Fuck!" a different soldier's scream was heard.

"I'm hit, I'm hit, Jesus, I'm hit," the first soldier still cried.

"Stay down, stay down," Mason heard another yelling.

The duck began to list, leaning to the port side as though trying to help shield its occupants. Hank reached up to turn the wheel, to steer the vehicle into its momentum and keep it straight.

"We're taking on water," Hank said over the droning of the engine. "We need to get to land."

"Stay down," Mason replied. "We're still in their range."

Hank reached up and flicked several switches. The flood lights overhead and the running lights around the duck went out.

"What do we do now?" O'Farrell asked.

"Stay down," Mason told them, edging to the rail in a crouching position. He began to wonder how many rounds he had left, if any.

Twenty-Six

A barrage of bullets struck the rear and side of the duck. Mason dropped to his chest. Half of the shots fired made no contact with the duck. He counted the sound of the guns firing against the swats over the duck and figured they had lost sight and were spraying in the area. It didn't mean it wasn't dangerous.

"Kill the engine," Mason said to Hank.

"I'll lose control," Hank objected.

"They can't see us. They only hear us."

"Shit," Hank grumbled as he let off on the gas. He reached a hand to the dash and turned the key. "We may not be able to start her," were Hank's words as the engine sighed its last knocking chug.

The *whit-dit-dit-dit* of two machine guns continued to fire, but the pelting of the vehicle eased almost immediately. One swatting of bullets came across the roof rack, then a second line of fire chewed at the aft deck, but then for as many streams of bullets that were fired, nothing came.

"Stay down," Mason warned them. Even though they weren't being hit, the machine guns were still directing fire into the channel.

"We've got to get the engine running," Hank said. "Do you feel it? We're tipping. We need the engine to straighten up or we're going to sink."

They continued to drift with the current and even Mason, whose head swam with dizziness, realized the port side was dipping further into the channel.

"All right," Mason agreed reluctantly. "Start her up."

Hank didn't climb out of his hiding hole. He reached up to the key and turned it. The glow plugs began to hum beneath the deck.

"Please start," O'Farrell moaned. "I can barely swim."

The engine whirred and chugged to life in one crank. Hank turned the wheel as he pressed the gas pedal. The duck straightened out and began to level off.

Mason looked up over the railing to see the island behind them, still glowing orange under a hundred small, unchecked fires. The toppled bridges were beyond his own firing range, but they were in range of those rifles.

"Stay down, Doc," Mason told O'Farrell.

Hank lifted his head above the dashboard to see ahead. The waterline was black, but the trees along the shore appeared in grey silhouettes that held up the night sky and all its stars. Hank veered the duck abruptly, tipping it more, turning it to port in an effort to drive straight at shore.

"Whoa," O'Farrell exclaimed as she fell sideways.

"Sorry, lady," Hank said. "We need to get to shore."

"Why are you heading *for* the Plagued States?" she asked as she crawled half of the way out from under the dashboard. Water was collecting in the foot well, dousing her pants.

"I don't think we'll get the warmest of receptions in the Rurals right now," Hank told her.

"But there are *zombies* over here."

"Yup. And maybe that'll keep those other bastards from looking for us," Hank said as he turned the wheel again, leveling the duck as it drove straight for shore. The current of the channel carried them further from the burning island. Mason sat up, relieved that they were now far enough out of range of the rifles. He saw the men on the remnants of the bridge carrying their injured colleagues toward the light of the Jeep parked there.

They didn't even know why they had been ordered to shoot at Mason and the others. They were just holding the bridge as they had probably been ordered, afraid that the vehicle contained infected people trying to reach the Rurals—their worst fear.

"Can we get up?" O'Farrell asked Mason.

"Sure," Mason told her wearily.

She climbed out of cover and sat in the chair alongside Hank, who was struggling to climb out from under the steering wheel.

"I want to go home. I want to go to *that* side," O'Farrell insisted, pointing behind them as she glared at Hank.

"Swim for it," Hank told her, not looking her way. He stood and looked over the windshield to gauge in the dark where they might reach land.

"What does that mean?" O'Farrell glowered. "Jones, are you hearing this?"

"I am," Mason said weakly, pushing the palms of his hands into his eyes. The pistol stood between him and his own skin. He held it in front of himself and the inkling of a memory rattled in his head, but he couldn't quite make it out. He knew it was a memory he feared, that one that gnawed at his dreams, kept him awake, haunted him for months before he ever came here. It was the memory that landed him in the hospital for evaluation, the place from which he had been plucked. And it was missing.

"Jones?" O'Farrell asked, looking at him worriedly. She slid out of her chair and crawled next to him. Hank looked over his shoulder with mild concern.

"You OK, kid?" Hank asked.

"What's wrong, Jones?" O'Farrell asked, a

reassuring hand on his shoulder.

"He wasn't the first soldier I've killed," Mason admitted. "That kid on the bridge," he added for clarification. He didn't mean Chavez. Mason hadn't actually killed Chavez as much as abandoned him anyway. "Before they shipped me here, I was in a psych ward. I mean I'm fine, I wasn't crazy or anything. I just couldn't cope. I mean, it's one thing to kill an enemy, but one of your own—"

"Jones," O'Farrell said softly.

"They're just holes. I can't remember my Christmas presents, or my girlfriend in high school. She exists. I know I had one. I'm not crazy."

"Jones, you're not crazy," O'Farrell assured him. "You're the first person who has been cured while in transition. Everyone else we've cured was already a full-fledged zombie. Basic language skills have to be taught to them all over again. Their minds are wiped clean, but for you, you're still mostly intact.

"Some of your memories may be gone, though. Permanently."

"I used to wish I could forget," Mason said. "I don't know what's worse."

The engine of the duck revved.

"Hey, hey, I found us a beach," Hank said excitedly. "We're not going to drown after all."

"Great," O'Farrell said cheerlessly. "Out of the frying pan, into the fire."

"You're looking at it all wrong, lady. In three days, we'll be at Biter's Bend and getting out of this shit hole once and for all."

"How are you going to manage that?" O'Farrell asked skeptically.

"Let's just say I know someone there who owes me a big favor," Hank replied with a wide smile.

"How big?" Mason wondered aloud.

"About as big as the one you owe me, kid," Hank said. "And he's got connections in all the right places." Hank began whistling as he turned the wheel again to level the deck. The continued jostling of the duck reminded Mason of his nausea and light-headedness. Hank continued turning the wheel to keep them facing shore, then turning it the other way to level them off. They lurched side to side.

"I'm going to be sick," Mason announced as he reached for the railing cable. He dry heaved over the side as O'Farrell held onto his waist. When he slumped back, he shoved his pistol into its holster and collapsed onto his back.

"Jones," O'Farrell asked as she tapped his face with the palm of her hand.

Her fingers were so cold, he thought.

"Jones, don't pass out on me."

"Doc, I got you out alive, right?" he said weakly, his eyes blinking as dark spots chewed away at his periphery.

She stared down on him with worried eyes, but nodded. "Lieutenant," O'Farrell said sharply.

Mason was so tired. His body had reached its limit; his mind had been stretched as far as it could go. He closed his eyes and wondered if his nightmare still lurked somewhere inside. He hoped it was there. At least it would remind him of who he was.

Jones, Mason E., Lieutenant, Army Ranger, Expert Marksmanship Badge in Pistol and Small-Bore Pistol. After serving 26 months in Egypt, he returned to the United States for clinical evaluation and to enroll in a mental health treatment program following an incident in which he was forced to take the life of one of his own soldiers under his command. After receiving a medical evaluation of minimal risk, he was assigned to the Rock Island Prison Defense Facility to serve out his remaining five months of active duty. At Rock Island, he was wounded by a subject infected with the consumption pathogen. Soon after, he caused a facility-wide prison escape. In the ensuing chaos, he evaded capture by his fellow soldiers, killing several, and directly caused the sentry ring to be utilized in defense of the country. He was last seen entering the Plagued States. His current whereabouts are unknown.

All went black and quiet.

The End

Stay up to date.
Follow us on Twitter *@BetterHeroArmy*,
or on the web at *www.betterheroarmy.com*

Other Stories by Better Hero Army

Nine Hours 'Till Sunrise
ISBN-13: 978-1492749479

When six desperados hunting their ex-partner ride into what appears to be a ghost town at dusk, they must fight to survive the night with the town's only two survivors, a woman and her deaf daughter, while fending off the animated bodies of the victims of a mysterious gas leak in the nearby mines.

Plagued: The Midamerica Zombie Half-Breed Experiment
Book 1 of the Plagued States of America series
ISBN-13: 978-1491216286

When Tom, the son of a powerful Senator, becomes stranded in the Plagued States of America while searching for his lost sister, his only hope of survival rests in the hands of a few grizzled veteran zombie hunters and a mysterious half-breed zombie woman he thinks may know where to find his sister.

Made in the USA
San Bernardino, CA
21 April 2014